SALTY CHICKS & SWEET LICKS

SA'ID SALAAM

Sa'id Salaam Presents

© 2018 Sa'id Salaam Presents Salty Chicks and Sweet Licks

Email: blackinkpublications1@gmail.com

Facebook: Black Ink Publications Like Page

Cover design: Sunny Giovonni

Edited by: Tisha Andrews

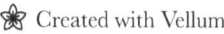 Created with Vellum

Chapter 1

"Ayo, Neek," Reign called when she spotted the Jamaican man named Rankin around the corner. The grown man had been flirting and outright propositioning the teen for weeks now.

"I see his blood clot, ras clot ass," Unique said with a snarl on her cute face.

The sixteen-year-old still had chubby kid cheeks, but glimpses of the pretty woman she would one day be could be seen under the acne and oil on her face. Her short hair stayed gelled down to her head since she didn't have any money to do anything else with it. Her lady curves were covered with baby fat, but were all there. She eased back into the building and found a hiding space where she coiled like a cobra, ready to strike.

Lately, Rankin started offering Reign cold, hard cash for some of her tight teen pussy. They settled on five hundred dollars. This was a fortune to a poor black girl from the notorious High Bridge section of the Bronx. She was street enough to know how her ass looked in the tiny shorts she wore since all the youngins in the hood were trying to get under the tiny shorts. She was still naive enough to wonder what a grown man would see in her.

Five hundred was nothing to Rankin since he was the weed man who supplied the west side of the Bronx. His posse controlled the weed in the whole borough, but this was his section. Reign's older brother Reef was the middleman who distributed the herbs on his behalf. Rankin would drop off the pounds of weed and come back to collect pounds of money. Reef had no idea he was using five hundred of it to fuck his sister.

"Whata gwan. Come 'ere gal with dat sweet poom poom," he beckoned and dug into his pocket to retrieve the cash. He licked his thick, blunt smoking blackened lips in anticipation. He planned to suck on her young poom poom once he got her up to the roof.

"We can go in my building," Reign said, pointing at a building she didn't live in. She had seen plenty sex acts on the tenement stairs and on the roof. She planned to let Kidd bust her cherry, but he got busted and sent to juvenile a few months back. She was loyal to her first boyfriend and decided to hold out for him despite dudes cracking about it every time she left.

"Look 'pon da sweetness," he said in his pronounced Patois and grabbed her fat ass jiggling in front of him. It was so firm yet soft, making him hard instantly. He was glad she bit on five hundred dollars because he would have paid more if he had to.

"Chill!" Reign fussed with a whine in her voice. She let Kidd grip her booty and finger fuck her, but the feel of the grown man's touch repulsed her. She broke into a semi-sprint to rush up the stairs. Rankin's eyes locked on her ass cheeks when the little shorts rose up, displaying her nice, round brown flesh. It made him sprint too to keep up.

R eign bust through the door leading to the roof with Rankin on her heels. She knew what was coming, closing her eyes as she ducked.

"Ugh!" Unique grunted as she swung an empty 40-ounce malt liquor bottle. The bottle didn't bust, but Rankin's eye did. A nasty gash opened over his eye as he went down on one knee. Unique swung the bottle again and collided with the back of his head. His thick dread locks saved his skull from being cracked, but he fell face down. His grip on the money loosened and she pulled it from his crusty hand and took off.

"Yo, you a'ight, B?" Reign asked and rushed to his side. She grimaced when he looked up with blood gushing from the wound over his eye. A gash on the back of his head leaked just as badly turning him wet and red from his own blood.

"Blood clot!" he fussed and cussed at the sight of his life liquid leaking from him.

"Who draw mi blood clot blood? Him a dead!"

"Some dude pushed me down and jumped on you!" she said, helping him to his feet. She grimaced once more when the blood got on her clothes. She sucked it up and helped him to the door since she had some money coming her way to go shopping.

"Yo, what the fuck?" Reef wanted to know when he saw his little sister helping the bloody dred out of the building.

"Some nigga jumped him on the roof!" Reign proclaimed.

"Who?" Reef frowned curiously. Everyone on the block knew who the Jamaican was, so he couldn't figure out who would rob him.

"One of them niggas from 170th, I think," she said to divert attention a few blocks away to a rival crew. 170th street was technically only six blocks away from 164, but a long-standing beef kept them as distant as North and South Korea. It wasn't a war where rivals shot on sight, but they just didn't fuck with each other. That is except Kidd and Reign. They weren't quite Romeo and Juliet, but Reef wouldn't let anyone on the block even look at his sister. So she had to go a few blocks up to find what would pass for love in High Bridge.

"Dem bust mi head! Stole mi money! I want revenge! I swear by Jah no more work until my blood is avenged!" Rankin vowed and stumbled to his car. He scraped one car and bumped another as he pulled off the block.

"The fuck?" Reef squinted at his sister. She raised her shoulders in a shrug as if she had no idea.

"Yo, what happened?" Unique asked as she came back outside. She had already changed clothes just in case Rankin saw her. Reign took notice of how good an actress her friend was. If she didn't see her just bust the man's head herself, she would have went for her act.

"Some dude from 170th bust Rankin's head!" Melody rushed in to answer. Reign smiled inwardly since the lie had grown legs. It would be law in an hour or so as it spread throughout the hood.

"Word?" Unique exclaimed quite believably. She and Reign shared a glance and smirk. Her brother met with the goons on the block to figure out their next move. Rankin said no more work until his blood was avenged. He just dropped off several pounds, but that would be it until they found out who robbed their connect. Coming on their block and robbing the connect was a violation in and of itself and had to be dealt with. Meanwhile, Reign and Unique had left to go shopping.

———

"Yooo, check this!" Reign gushed and fawned over a red mini dress. She plucked it off the rack and pressed it against her firm body. "Kidd gone love seeing me in this bad bitch!"

"Yup and Reef gone lose his damn mind," Unique reminded. She was lucky enough not to have an older brother who would dictate what she could and could not wear and who she could or could not date. As a result she dressed in skimpy clothing and had sex with a few dudes on the block. Her only worry was her ratchet mother wearing her clothes or smoking her weed.

"What he don't see won't hurt him," Reign said and put the dress in her basket.

It was small enough to conceal under her clothes to get out of the house. Her brother had a fit about the little shorts she wore to lure Rankin to the rooftop. She had to change anyway since they had his blood on them. Now they spent the spoils of their lick. It was their first, but it was so easy and so lucrative that it wouldn't be their last. School was weeks away, so they wisely bought jeans, boots and sweatshirts to prepare for the rough New York winter right around the corner.

They bought matching sneakers and airbrushed shirts for the last block party of the summer. Last stop was a slum jewelry store for matching earrings so they could stunt on their class-mates. The two fifty each went a long way in the hood stores on Fordham Road.

Both had single mothers who would do what they could to buy school clothes for them, but if they wanted to be fly they would have to grow wings. Their mothers would buy school supplies, mismatched panties and bras along with basic clothes and shoes. Since they did want to be fly, that licked allowed them to grow wings, robbing on the connect that flooded their neighborhood with drugs..

"Yo, we gotta throw these receipts away!" Reign remem-bered as the bus neared the block. Everyone knew the girls didn't have money of their own to shop with, so they had no business with receipts.

"Word!" Unique quickly agreed and discarded hers. Boosting wasn't just acceptable, it was expected.

Reign's eyes turned on their own as they passed by 170th street. She let out a lovesick sigh as she thought of Kidd. She snarled at the girls on his block wondering which one of them liked her boyfriend. Quite a few of them did since he was quite the playboy. He ran through his own block and then spread throughout High Bridge.

"Girl, let me find out you sprung!" Unique teased when she saw a lovesick glow in her friend's eyes.

"Nuh uh!" she shot back, giggled then came clean. "Un huh. I can't wait for that nigga to come home!"

"So, you gone fuck him?" her friend asked, causing an older lady to snap her head in their direction. "Uh, mind yo' business!"

"You crazy!" Reign laughed to change the subject away from her virginity. Hers was the last remaining cherry of their class, mainly because her overly protective brother who wouldn't let anyone get close to her. Reef was a known shooter and no one wanted to get shot. Especially since Unique was generous with her vagina.

"Okay, crazy," she shot back knowingly. She reached up and pressed the strip to signal the driver to stop on their block. The bus came to a hissing stop and the girls got off.

"Uh oh! Y'all bitches hit the block, I see!" Neta cheered when she saw their arms full of bags. Then saw the cheap 10k gold nameplates on their necks. "Man, why y'all ain't take me?"

"How 'bout cuz you got caught last time!" Reign shot back. The reason was valid, so she fell back.

"But we can smoke one with you," Unique threw in to change the subject from their clothes.

"Bet!" she said, accepting the charity. She fell in step behind the girls and followed them into Reign's building to put their bags down. Then they headed to Unique's apartment since they couldn't smoke in Reign's. Her hardworking mother didn't approve of the girls smoking, but Unique's mom didn't mind as long as she could get a pull or two off the blunt.

"Let me holla at Seven," Unique said since he was her first. She assumed giving him her virginity a couple months back would be good for a free bag. She could save her ten bucks for tomorrow's weed, since tomorrow's weed isn't promised.

"You heard what happened to Rankin?" Neta asked urgently, hoping to be the first to spread some gossip.

"Nah, what?" she asked to see what the story had morphed into. Gossip had a crazy way of changing as it passed from person to person. Everyone added a little themselves as they handed it off to the next ear waiting to hear.

"That dude Big C from 170th bust his head and stole five thousand dollars from him!" she reported.

"Dang!" Reign shot back with genuine awe at how much it had grown. She watched her friend switch her ample ass over to Seven posted up on his stoop. The pretty seventeen-year-old thug munched chips and sipped on a quarter water while smoking a menthol.

"Hey, Seven," Unique sang and stood over him with her crotch in his face as a reminder.

"What's up, yo?" he asked glancing at her crotch, face, back to her crotch, then away. He once liked her enough to "go with her", but she fucked a few guys right after him and he lost interest.

"Let me get a fat dime," she purred. There was a brief, silent standoff when neither reached. She didn't reach for money, so he didn't reach for the weed.

"Ten bucks, yo," he reminded her of the cost of a dime bag.

"Oh yeah? Okay," she relented and dug into her pocket. Easier said than done since her shorts were so tight they rendered the pockets to being almost useless. Reign watched and learned a tacit lesson that vagina is worth way more before you give it away than after. Unique had sex with him and it didn't get her a ten-dollar bag of weed while the promise of some pussy cost Rankin five hundred bucks.

"Here you go," Seven said as they traded dope for dollars. He was nonchalant when she was in his face, but her departure had his full attention. He bit his bottom lip as he watched her fat ass shift from side to side.

"You stupid!" Reign laughed as her friend put on a booty shaking display.

"Nah, letting him see what he can't never get!" she shot back, minus saying "anymore" since everyone knew he already got it. So did Charles, Black and Tito, but lately she started saying no to everyone. She was in high demand once word got out that she was putting out. Lately, she cut off the traffic to her brand new vagina.

"Mmhm," both Neta and Reign both hummed since they both knew and cracked up. She lifted her pretty chin and led the way up to her apartment.

"Who dat?" Unique's mother Simone called from her bedroom when she heard the front door open and close. It was rhetorical since the two of them lived alone. The 32-year-old mother had more ass than brains and said silly shit like that on a regular basis. She wasn't quite sure which one of the men her mother dealt with fathered her, but she definitely got her smarts from him.

"It's me, ma!" she called back. "You smoking?" Simone suddenly appeared like a magic trick at the mention of free smoke. The girls got a good giggle out of it and passed her the cigar since she still rolled the tightest, neatest blunts on the block. Reign helped herself and turned on the stereo to fill the sparse apartment with music.

"Yo, Marcus 'sposed to give me some money to take you school shopping," Simone advised and lit the weed.

"Bet," she cheered. If she had a choice of fathers, it would have been him. He had a respectable job at the post office and nothing bad could be said about the man. He didn't buy drugs from any of the dope boys nor solicit booty from any of the thots on the block. He had a thing for Simone but she was still too immature to overlook his overweight.

"I like Mr. Marcus!" Neta announced and Reign cosigned

with a nod. He often paid for their pizza if he ever caught them in the pizza shop and never tried to fuck them like some grown men.

"He's a'ight," Simone sang like she was 16 too. They smoked, danced and gossiped about everyone on the block. Nightfall fell, so it was time for Reign to get home. Her mother worked the overnight shift at Lincoln Memorial Hospital and wanted her daughter home before she left.

"I gotta bounce," she announced and stood.

"Ma, I'ma spend the night with Reign," Unique announced with enough reflection in her tone for it to be counted as a question.

"Again?" Simone asked, sounding slightly wounded at being left out. She would have hung out and spent the night with the girls too if she could. Had Reign asked, she would have packed a bag and came along with them. Neta would have too, but wasn't invited either.

"Mmhmm," she said, breaking off a few buds from her bag of weed. Getting high alone beat just being alone and sealed the deal.

"Okay, but don't y'all be having no boys over there!" she said like the good mother she could sometimes be. She didn't smoke crack or have men in and out of her house, so she could be a lot worse. She would hit the club and spend nights out though, so she could be a lot better.

"Don't worry, Miss Simone. My brother ain't gone let no niggas up in there!" Reign stated as a matter of fact.

"Oh okay. Guess I'm gone hit the club then," Simone said and wound her hips.

"See you tomorrow, ma," Unique said and went to retrieve a change of clothes. Her mother hit the shower to get ready for a night on the town.

Chapter 2

"Mmhm," Sharon hummed and glanced up at the wall clock when Reign and Unique walked in a few ticks before she had to leave for work. Her curfew was ten when she was home, but it moved back an hour on the nights Sharon had to work.

"Hey, ma. What you cooked?" she asked and kissed her cheek before checking the pots.

"Mmhmm," her mother hummed again to let her know she could smell the weed on her. She knew fussing about her daughter smoking weed when her son was selling it was futile, but she wasn't going to stop.

"Yes! Chicken and dumplings!" Reign sang and danced, ignoring her mother's subtle complaint.

"Oh, I love your chicken and dumplings, Miss Sharon!" Unique cheered and grabbed a bowl.

"If you staying over here tonight, ain't no in and out!" she fussed like she did every night. She and Simone were friendly, but not exactly friends. Unique's mother was too immature to really be friends, but since their daughters were best friends, she had a vested interest in Unique, as well. Sharon worked at the nearest hospital so she saw plenty of kids from the block at the attached STD clinic. Not to mention a mean teen pregnancy rate.

"OK, ma. No boys!" Unique mocked at what she knew was coming next.

"That's right! No boys," she said anyway. Keeping boys out of her home was a good start to keeping boys out of her daughter. That was the least of her worries since her son Reef wouldn't let that happen anyway. Both kids were allowed company, but Reef had an old school chivalry about him, not allowing any guys around his mother or sister.

"Have a good night at work, ma," Reign sang and kissed her mother's cheek once again as she left the apartment.

She rushed to the window to watch her walk up the block to the bus like she had done since she was a little girl. The bus stop was around the corner, so she couldn't see her board, but she always knew she was on the next one headed down the hill to Yankee Stadium.

"Roll up!" Unique demanded when she turned back out the window. She pulled the weed from her pocket, but quickly tucked it away when the door opened.

"Ma left?" Reef asked even though he knew she should have. He just wanted confirmation before ducking into her bedroom.

"Just left," Reign replied to her brother as he playfully punched Unique in her arm on his way through the living room.

"Stop playing, punk!" she shot back trying to play mad, but cracked up. She was just one of many local girls who had a crush on the handsome twenty-year-old. None more than his baby mama, Lisa.

Reef didn't have time to chitchat and entered his mother's locked bedroom. Sharon only used the flimsy lock so her nosey kids would have to go through the motions of picking it with a butter knife. He locked it behind him and rushed into her closet. He pulled the shoeboxes out and lifted up the floorboards. He grabbed the dirty .38 from inside and put in his pocket before putting the closet back together and leaving.

"Give me a blunt, Reef," Reign demanded. He instantly reached into a pocket and tossed her a bag from his personal stash. "You giving me money to go school shopping?"

"Like I ain't heard y'all went boosting today. Came back with mad bags," he replied. It wasn't a no and they both knew he would break bread, so she left it alone and he left them alone.

"Save that regular weed for later. We 'bout to smoke this fruity," Reign announced and held up the colorful, fluffy buds. This was different than the commercial grade weed the dealers on the block dealt.

"Hello!" Unique greeted the suggestion and got to rolling. The girls blazed up while watching DVDs and munching on whatever they could find.

"I'm 'bout to take my shower," Reign announced when her yawns grew deeper and longer. She did just that and changed into hood pajamas of t-shirt and panties.

"My turn," Unique said as soon as she stepped out. She too showered and changed into her own t-shirt and panties.

"No homo," Reign chuckled when Unique climbed in her bed. They'd been saying it since they were five years old since they've been sharing a bed for that long. Making a pallet on the floor was out unless you don't mind sleeping with mice. Miss Sharon would fuss if she caught someone sleeping on her sofa. It hadn't been new anymore for years, but she still fussed like it was.

"No homo," Unique repeated between a yawn and blinked herself to sleep.

———

"Yo, Unique," Reef whispered and pulled her foot. He froze momentarily when his sister stirred. Reign flipped over and began snoring lightly. He reached up Unique's legs and patted the plump mound between her legs. "Neek."

"Hmph?" she asked as she awoke. She blinked Reef into focus and eased out of the bed. They crept out the room and eased the door closed so it wouldn't make any noise.

"Come on," he said as they entered his room. She climbed on the bed while he stepped out his expensive sneakers and jeans. He was so eager to get inside her that his erection popped through the hole in his boxers. Unique stifled a girlish giggle looking at his dick. She lifted her hips slightly to help him remove her wet cotton panties with cartoon characters on them.

"Damn, girl," Reef exclaimed when he fondled her nearly new vagina and it instantly soaked his fingers. The silly teens she let hit made the mistake of declaring it the best pussy on the block. Not that they had sampled all the pussy on the block. Reef did and had been up in almost everything in age range 17 to 30. He had to try it out for himself and it was better than they said it was. He started hitting her a couple weeks ago and made her stop giving it to anyone else.

"Yessss," she replied to a probing finger sliding in and out of her. The tightness made his dick throb, so he took position between her legs. Unique braced herself by gripping handfuls of his sheets as he rubbed his swollen dick head between her slippery lips. Another cry escaped when he eased his way inside her hot young vagina.

"Shit," he cursed when he realized he wasn't going to last long inside of her. In general, he was no slouch in the sack, but this brand new box always got the best of him. He and Lisa could fuck for hours, but he couldn't last in Unique no more than a couple minutes at a time. "Mmmm."

"Okay now, be careful," she warned when his moans grew louder and his strokes slowed to deep grinds. She knew what followed since he came inside of her the last few times they were together.

"Shit," he repeated, but didn't repeat his mistake and snatched out of her at the last second, exploding on her belly. Unique leaned up and watch globs of warm semen paint her stomach. He collapsed on top of her and gasped for air. "Shit!"

"Mmmm, that was so good!" she purred and rubbed his back. It was actually more pain than pleasure, but he was pleased and that pleased her. She wished they could fall asleep just like that now and forever, but knew what was coming.

"A'ight, ma," he sighed, wishing he could go to sleep right there on top of her.

He would fuck her real good in the morning with that good morning piss hard on, but he had to go. Besides, he'd been chasing dicks away from his sister the second after she grew titties and her ass rounded out, so it would be a huge contradiction if he were sexing her friend who was the same age. Can't really tell her not to fuck if he was fucking her best friend.

"I know," she moaned and mourned her loss when he lifted his fine brown frame off her body. To her surprise, he leaned down and kissed her for the first time. Her shock intensified when he slid his tongue into her mouth. He swirled it around her mouth until his erection throbbed to life once more. His dick stiffened up next when he did that, causing him to slide back inside of her.

Reef and Unique kissed feverishly as he dug her young ass out with low, slow strokes. The tongue in her mouth prevented the next warning when he began to moan again. Obviously he needed that warning because without it he pushed against her cervix and exploded.

"I gotta get back out on the block," he explained almost apologetically.

"I know, baby," she replied, feeling quite grown at the moment. She pulled her panties back on and rolled out of his bed. He cracked the door and peeked out to make sure the coast was clear. It was, so he hopped across to the bathroom to wash his dick in the sink. Unique slipped back into Reign's room and slid back in bed. Reign was still snoring lightly and she quickly joined her.

———

"**D**ang girl, you sleeping all hard! Slobbering and whatnot," Reign fussed playfully as she shook her friend awake the next morning.

"Mmm, I was sleeping good, too!" Unique moaned and stretched. The movement made her sore vagina throb, reminding her why she slept so well. A sly smile spread on her face thinking of the thug loving she got in the middle of the night.

"Come on, girl. My moms in the kitchen. Let's catch her before she go to bed," Reign said urgently.

Neither girl could cook, so they hoped to get a home cooked meal. Sharon gave up on trying to teach Reign how to cook because she showed no interest in it. She would either play around or pout until Sharon ran her out her kitchen. Simone tried to teach her daughter to cook as well, but she wasn't a very cook herself. She knew the way to a man's heart is through his stomach. That's just one way though because some bomb ass head works just as well.

"Hey, ma!" both girls sang and kissed opposite sides of Sharon's cheeks.

"Mmhmm," she hummed and twisted her lips knowingly. She reached back into the fridge and retrieved the bacon, eggs and a can of biscuits.

"These too, ma!" Reign requested and pulled hash browns from the freezer.

"You girls really need to learn how to cook! How you expect to keep a man one day?" she grumbled, but took the potatoes to cook.

"Hmph!" both girls huffed knowing it would be their vaginas keeping a man. They were young and dumb enough to believe pussy can keep a man.

"Girl, every female on the planet got a vagina. Don't think that will hold him!" she advised them as if she could hear their thoughts.

"But mom, you a dope cook," Reign said, trying to see why her mother didn't have a man. She was smart, pretty, good job and great cook, but never brought any man around.

"How about because I don't want one? I ain't got time for all that," she said and rattled off a few more excuses that didn't add up. She was saved when Reef came out of his room.

"What's up, ma. Big head and bigger head," he greeted his mother and teased the girls. Unique looked at his shirtless torso and felt her pussy throb once again. She drifted down and gawked at his crotch area.

"Reef put a shirt on around these girls! And me 'cause no one wanna see your bird chest," the fussy mother fussed.

"Okay, ma," he laughed and snagged a piece of bacon from the paper towel she used to sop up the grease. He retreated back to the bathroom to shower so he could hit the block. The girls and Sharon were enjoying a good breakfast when Reef returned.

"Here, for school," he said, handing Reign a wad of cash. Unique got a smaller wad of cash, too. "You too, bigger head."

"Thank you!" they both sang while Sharon turned away and pretended not to see her son give her daughter drug money for school shopping. It pained her not to be able to do more and she didn't expect them to go without. So she turned a blind eye to his means of supporting his family.

Reef hit the door and hit the block. Sharon went to bed and the girls got dressed to go back to Fordham Road to buy more clothes. They planned to be the baddest chicks on the block and school.

Chapter 3

U nique was greeted by sounds of sex when she walked into her apartment before heading out to shop. She told Reign she needed to check on her mom, but really wanted a quick shower so she could change out of the cum-crusted panties she woke up in.

"Dang, ma," she giggled hearing Simone's moans and head-board slamming into the wall. Whoever he was, was beating it up so good the skin slapping echoed in the quiet apartment. She quietly eased into the shower and washed the sex away.

"My daughter is here," Simone warned her guest once she heard the water turn on. Her vaginal guest slowed down his stroke and dug in. Deep slow grinding strokes that propelled them both over the edge. She clamped her mouth with her own hand and busted a good nut.

"Ugh, shit! Whew!" he grunted and grinded as he filled his condom.

"Hey, Bryan—" she began and squeezed her internal muscles, lovingly rubbing his back.

"Bryan," he cut in and corrected her. Not that it mattered since he conquered what he came for. He went to the club last night looking for exactly what he got. A fine, easy chick with her own apartment.

"That's right. I always be adding a 't'," she giggled from embarrassment before she continued. "Can I borrow some money? It's for my daughter. School's about to start and—"

"Pass me my pants," he said. He marveled at her marvelous ass as she went to retrieve his slacks. Her plump vagina popped out from between her round ass cheeks when she bent over. He shook his head at the missed opportunity to hit her from the back. She handed them over and he parted with a crisp hundred-dollar donation.

"Thank you," Simone said appreciatively. She shut down the booty show momentarily when she wrapped in a robe and rushed from the room. She walked briskly down the hall to Unique's room.

"Hey, ma. Don't worry, I'm 'bout to bounce. I know you got company," Unique announced when Simone opened her bedroom door and stuck her head inside. She never knocked since she paid the rent.

"Oh, you good. We were just talking. Anyway, here's a little something for clothes. Clothes, Unique! Not weed or bullshit!" she warned her. Unique wasn't used to money and people not used to money are quick to fuck it up on frivolous shit.

"Okay, ma. Just clothes. Thank you," she said and hopped up to kiss her cheek. "Love you, ma!"

"Love you too, chica," Simone smiled and bolted back to her room. Bryan was sliding his pants on when she arrived. "You leaving?"

"Yeah, I have to get home," he nodded, leaving out the part of his wife and kids. Not that Simone would have cared. He just laid some mean pipe and broke bread. He was welcome any time he wanted to come over and make her cum.

"But I didn't get a chance to thank you," she whined and rubbed his crotch. She felt him jump then stiffen as she removed his meat from his pants.

"Mmmm, you're welcome," Bryan moaned when the hot mouth engulfed him. Simone settled on her knees and worked her neck like she wanted him to cum and come back. When his leg began to buck and buckle, she knew he would do both.

"Mmmm, shit," Bryan moaned. Simone snatched him out of her mouth and finished him off with her hand and the saliva she left behind. She opened her robe and let him bust on her pretty breast. A lady never swallows on the first date.

"So, you gonna come back and see me?" she pouted, feeling his warm semen running down her torso. She looked up and batted her pretty brown eyes at him and sealed the deal.

"Tomorrow!" he quickly replied. He was in the market for a new side chick and may have just found her.

———

"What took you so long?" Reign asked when Unique finally came back downstairs. She filled the void by letting Tito flirt with her while shaking her head 'no' the whole time. He was flirting with death too, since Reef was dead serious about his little sister.

"My mom gave me a yard!" she said instead of 'your brother came in me last night and I had to take a shower'. It was late summer, so she couldn't run around with sex residue in her panties.

"Well, let's go get fly on these hoes!" Reign said triumphantly. She didn't dress just to look good for herself. She dressed to impress.

"Oh, they gone hate us!" she agreed. The first day of school was always a fashion show. Every girl on their block and every other block were doing whatever they needed to do to get school clothes.

Once again, the girls went uptown to Fordham Road for clothes. And again the girls were smart enough to think ahead to the fast approaching winter. New York winters come quick and hard for the unprepared.

"Oh, look at those jeans! And they buy one get one free!" Unique pointed at a store window. Reign had to jog to keep up. They often dressed alike because they were besties and because of buy one get one free.

"Girl, you need to sign up for track 'cause—" Reign complained, but stopped short when she saw a group of girls at the sneaker section.

Unique frowned curiously and followed Reign's eyes to see what caught her attention. Leticia Lazaro lived in the same building as Kidd and went to the same school. Kidd denied ever messing with the girl, but she heard otherwise. Besides, Leticia wouldn't be turning her nose up at her right now if they hadn't.

"She look like a lab rat," Unique laughed at her high yellow complexion. Leticia was actually quite funny looking, but had a banging body and was light skin. That was enough for the dudes to come sniffing behind her and her having the attitude that came along with all the attention.

"Damn albino," Reign laughed. She made sure to yuck it up real good so the girl knew she was laughing at her. They glared at each other for a moment then resumed shopping. They both made sure not to select what the other selected since they did not want to be caught wearing matching outfits. Never mind that they were buying clothes off the rack. Everywhere they went in the city, someone would be wearing the same thing.

"She must want beef. She don't want no beef!" Unique said loudly as Leticia and her friends exited the store with their clothing.

"Nah, she don't want nothing," she replied gladly. She didn't either since she had the boy that the beef was about. It was Leticia's problem, not hers. "But if she ever try me, I'ma give her yellow ass some colors."

"Word up! We gone turn that bitch black, blue, red and purple!" Unique laughed. They spent most of their money, but made sure to save some for calzones, weed and wine coolers for when they got back to the block. They were all set for school. Now all that was left was the end of summer block party.

———

"What's up?" Reef asked when he walked into the apartment and found Unique sitting on the sofa. He looked around to see who else was there in with hopes of running up in her real quick. He was quickly getting addicted to putting his dick in her.

"Hey," Unique blushed under his probing gaze. She felt a throb in her vagina as it threatened to get wet just from seeing him.

"Where Reign?" he asked wondering if he had a chance to smash real quick. The sofa was the scene of their first late night romp when Reign fell asleep during a movie.

"In the shower," she said just as Reign came out of the bathroom.

"I'm done," she announced so Unique could shower since she was getting dressed for the block party over there. Simone wore anything she found, so Unique kept most of her gear over here at Reign's house. "Oh, what's up, Reef?"

"Y'all coming to the party?" he asked more rhetorical than curious. Even Sharon knew her daughter was going to the last block party of the summer and relaxed her curfew rule.

"Hell yeah. Give us some weed?" she demanded but paused when she watched his eyes watch her friend's ass as she walked down the hallway into the bathroom. "Let me find out you like young broads!"

"Huh? What? Girl, you bugging. Here!" he stammered and produced a bag of colorful weed from his personal stash.

He rushed from the room in embarrassment without warning her about the action he planned. Rankin came through to collect what he was owed but kept his word and wouldn't break them off until his blood was avenged. That meant Big C had to shed some blood of his own.

They had no proof he was the culprit but when the rumor reached Rankin they had no choice. If they wanted to eat he had to be put to sleep. The hood is funny like that sometimes, especially the Bronx where life was sex, money and murder.

"We gonna stunt on these bum bitches!" Reign declared when she and Unique finished dressing. They couldn't pass for twins since she was a few shades darker, but they still dressed alike.

"Say word!" Unique confirmed to their reflection.

Both wore tight jeans shorts and airbrushed t-shirts bearing their names. Matching sneakers and slum gold nameplates rounded out their outfits.

Reign had some fresh cornrows since Unique knew how to braid. She couldn't braid her own hair so it was gelled down to her scalp as always.

Nonetheless they accomplished their mission and were cute. They could have smoked their weed right there but then no one would have seen them. The main part of stunting on them is letting them see you.

———

"This gonna be popping!" Reign announced when they could hear music pumping as soon as they stepped on Ogden Avenue.

"Packed too," her friend agreed as she saw foreign faces making the trek over to Nelson Park where the jam was coming to life. The park's central location meant people from both 164th and 170th street would be in the same place at the same time. High Bridge was known to have the best block parties in the borough, so folks from the other 4 boroughs flocked to the park.

They were both right because the park was popping and packed when they arrived. The girls scanned the area in search of their own and made their way over to Neta and the flock of girls from the block. They were confidently posted within eyeshot of the pack of hoodrats from 170th. Both sides talked and laughed loud for attention. Both sides made a big deal out of swigging forty ounces and smoking blunts in rotation. Both sides talked about the other side, what they wore, and how they wore their hair.

"Bitch look like a tranny!" Leticia cracked at Unique's hair. She certainly couldn't call the cute girl 'ugly' so she cracked her hair.

Word!" her girls cosigned and laughed loudly.

"Bitch look like a white gerbil!" Unique cracked and her friends cracked up loudly. Meanwhile, Reign cocked her head and frowned curiously when she saw her brother's baby mama getting friendly with a guy. Not just any guy either.

"Big muthafucking C!" Lisa said, looking him up and down like a tasty snack. She was acting but he was a handsome six foot four inch hunk of thug.

"Sup Lisa," he replied and squinted down at her to see what she wanted. Her eyes settled back on his crotch causing him to twist his lips and ask, "Where's yo' baby daddy?"

"Reef don't own me! Just cuz we got a kid don't mean shit. I do what I want to do," she said and reached out to touch the bulge that wasn't there when she came over.

"So, what you tryna do, ma? Huh?" he asked and reached down and around to palm her fat ass. She let him feel it just enough to seal the deal before moving his hand away.

"The fuck!" Reign fussed when she saw the violation. She looked around the park for her brother hoping he would catch him in the act and bust his head.

"What girl?" Unique asked urgently when she saw the look on her face.

"Yo, this nigga is trying my brother," she growled. She really got hot when she saw Lisa take his hand and turn to leave the park.

"He ain't the only one! We should tell Reef!" Unique declared. She was all for Reef leaving Lisa so she could have him to herself. At least that's how it worked in her 16-year-old mind. She was still too young and dumb to understand no one woman could ever possess a man like Reef.

"Nah, I'm 'bout to beat them both up for tryna to play my brother. Come on," she said and took off behind them.

Chapter 4

"Neek, you sleep? Neek?" Reign asked and shook her friend to wake her up.

"Nah, man," she groaned and tried to roll over.

Reef had just woke her up a few hours ago when he got in and dicked her down real good. He got good and liquored up after the murder and lasted longer than usual. Probably because he warmed up in his baby mama before coming home.

It was as close as she'd come to coming in her young life. At this stage she got super turned on and crazy wet, but the actual act just hurt. She would just grit her teeth, grip the sheets and take it. As a result of the early morning loving, she was sore and throbbing.

"Yo, that was crazy last night!" she said, wide-eyed and full of excitement. Life in High Bridge was like an action movie. Someone was always getting fucked or fucked up. Shootouts happened on a regular, but seeing her brother gun the man down was indeed crazy.

"It was!" Unique agreed, but she meant the sex.

A soft smile spread on her face as she recalled how Reef reached around and gripped her ass and dug her out real deep and slow. They traded saliva as their tongues danced in each other's mouth while he made love to her. That too was a first since the three guys before him just humped and humped until they filled up their condom. She felt the flutters of orgasm building inside of her, but he grunted and exploded just before she got there. He bust inside of her once again, but he said it was his pussy so he could do whatever he wanted with it.

"Well, Big C shouldn't have done what he did," Reign said and lifted her head indignantly. She knew he died for something she did, but she could live with it.

"Word up," she agreed again because she could, too. Life wasn't fair in High Bridge and they accepted it. If life were fair they would have dads, money, futures, and most of all, wouldn't live in High Bridge. A knock on the door broke up the moment and Reign rushed to answer before whoever was knocking woke her mom up.

"Yooo! Y'all missed it! It was crazy!" Neta cheered as soon as Reign opened the door. She did a little gossip dance from foot to foot while she served the tea.

"Chill, yo. My moms just got in. She sleep," she fussed in a hush and ushered her inside. "Hole up, we 'bout to get dressed."

"Sup," Unique greeted when Neta stepped in.

"Yooo!" she began again in a whisper since she was eager to be the first one to spread gossip. Everyone who gossips always wants to be first to spread the news.

"Chill, yo!" Reign repeated and scrunched up her face. The last thing she needed was her brother or mother to hear about a murder first thing in the morning. Reef would be .38 hot to hear her discussing the murder he committed. It wasn't his first, but it was the first one anyone witnessed.

"My bad!" Neta whispered. "Y'all hurry up and get dressed."

"We can go to my crib. My mom should be at work," Unique suggested.

She was eager to shower the sex away before getting dressed. People could call her ratchet, but they couldn't call her dirty.

Her mother stressed the importance of keeping a clean, tidy vagina since she was little. She couldn't be called dumb either since she was actually quite smart. She was smarter than Reign, but smart enough not to let it show. Instead, she let her take the lead and played sidekick.

Reign wanted a shower too, but it would have to wait. She needed to hear what the streets were saying about the latest murder. The girls dressed and walked outside. The day shift dope boys were already out slinging weed. Reef ran the block and didn't allow crack to be sold on it. It was lucrative, but came with hella traffic and hella drama.

He wanted neither on his own block where his own mother and sister had to walk. The next thing would be crack-stitutes walking up and down the block renting out their nasty mouths and vaginas. Plenty of dudes from the block slung crack and/or heroin, they just didn't do it on the block. Including Reef, who had some youngins from the projects slinging for him since he didn't care about their mothers and sisters.

"Sup, Reign. Neta," Seven greeted noticeably leaving Unique out.

He was slightly salty about her sexing a couple dudes after him, but still wanted her. His biggest problem was he couldn't get it again. He had yet to realize it was him running his mouth about not just hitting it, but how good it was, that put Black, Tito and Charles on to her. He should have kept it to himself and could have kept it to himself.

"Humph," Unique huffed and lifted her chin proudly. Her tight little box was still full of Reef's seeds, so he wasn't talking about nothing.

"Let me get a blunt," Reign sang sweetly. The teen boy blushed and pulled a perfectly rolled blunt from behind his ear. "Thank you."

"Bet," he nodded and locked in on Reign's ass as they walked away. He glanced at Unique's, Neta's, then back to Reign's. All three had fat little butts, but he wanted Reign's.

"I'ma tap that."

"He like you," Neta stated the obvious. Reign was a pretty brown girl with plump breast and a fat ass so plenty dudes "liked" her.

"Yo, I got a man!" she shot back, meaning her boyfriend, Kidd.

"Yeah, but he locked up!" she shot back. Plenty of chicks in the hood had dudes who got locked up and they usually had another dude to keep it warm until they came back home. They were ride or lie chicks, not ride or die chicks.

"Girl, she not messing with no damn Seven!" Unique shot back in her friend's defense. Simone was rushing out the building just as they reached it. "Hey, ma. Thought you had to work?"

"I do. I'm late!" she said and rushed down the block to catch the bus. They rushed upstairs to smoke and hear what Neta had to say.

"OK, OK!" Neta said dramatically. "So check it. Mia 'sposed to go with Chuck, but Chuck was all pushed up on that Puerto Rican chick, Jennifer. Bitch think she J-lo cuz she Puerto Rican and from the Bronx! So anyway, Mia was like fuck him and pushed up on Vic. They went over to the playground to get it in and guess what they seen?"

Both girls shot each other a glance before turning to her and shrugging their shoulders. Each held their breath and awaited the news they knew was coming. More importantly they listened for what gossip and speculation came with it. They knew better than most that gossip and speculation can get you killed.

"What?" Reign and Unique asked, perfectly in sync as only best friends can.

"That dude Big C dead! He got shot like fifty-eleven times!" she said dramatically. Neta could have a real shot in Hollywood, but chances are she would never leave 164th Street. She was a second-generation hoe. And the by way she was fucking, a third generation wasn't far off. She too had a box full of dope boy cum in her right now from the after party, after the party. Tito bagged her from the park and sexed her in the staircase of her building once the jam was over.

"Word!" they exclaimed, still in chorus. Then Reign asked, "Who did it?"

"I'on know. They saying it was somebody from our block cuz they say Big C was the one robbed the dred for fifty g's," she said to their dismay.

"Ain't nobody from 164th did nothing to that nigga!" Reign said so forcefully Neta opened her mouth to ask how she knew. Luckily, fast thinking Unique jumped in to steer the conversation in another direction.

"Yo, it was probably them dreds! I seen like five of them in the park last night!" she said, showing off her acting skills.

"Word!" Neta said as she chomped on the bait. Reign shot Unique a grateful glance knowing she told the right one. Neta was the head gossiper on the block. Nine times out of ten, she was the "they" in "they said". She was the keeper of some of the community coochie, which meant she was in a lot of dudes' ears while they were in her.

"Anyway, you ready for school?" Reign asked to change the subject away from her brother's capital charge.

"Hell naw, but it don't matter," Neta shrugged. She didn't get many new clothes from her single mother. Welfare paid the bills around the apartment but there wasn't much left over. She was lucky to get school supplies and new underclothes.

"Nah, it don't matter," Unique echoed, since ready or not, school was a day away.

———

"My baby in the 11th grade!" Simone cheered when Unique appeared from the bathroom. She was cute too in a pink body hugging knit dress and matching Adidas.

"Which means I ain't no baby," she fussed. She was a grown woman now have her tell it since she was having sex now.

"You still my baby!" she assured her and forced some kisses on her chubby cheeks. The grown woman went out the window when she giggled and squealed like she did when she was three.

"Simone?" Bryan called from her bedroom door and stepped out into the hall. "I gotta get to work."

"Oh, OK," she said since the cat was out of the bag. She hoped to keep him a secret as long as she could. It was futile since Unique slept at home last night and heard them go three rounds. Bryan and Unique checked each other out as Simone made the introductions. "Unique, this my friend Bryant. Bryant, this my baby Unique."

"Bryan," he corrected once again. Sooner or later he was just going to have to get use to it and go by Bryant while he was over there. "Nice to meet you. Your mom tells me you're a straight A student."

"Yup," she said proudly. She saw his eyes run her up and down, but thought nothing of it since men, almost all men almost always did. "Ma, I need some lunch money."

"Dang, they don't have lunch at school no more?" Simone moaned as she went for her purse. Unique and Bryan looked each other up and down once more when she dipped into her room. She was thick, but had nothing on her mother. "Here you go."

"Thanks, ma," she smiled and kissed her mother's cheek. She should have gave Bryan one too since she got it from him. Then again, Simone already gave him his money's worth.

Simone saw Bryan glance at her daughter's ass as it jiggled down the hall and out the door. She did mind, but didn't want to run him off. A look wouldn't hurt anyone, she told herself and let it go. Unique's jiggling ass drew plenty of eyes as she made her way over to Reign's building where the rest of their little crew waited. Reef was the man on the block, so it was only right that his sister ran her peers.

"Sup, yo!" Neta greeted along with Aniqa, Treasure and Yvonne.

"Sup," she replied and struck a pose so they could check out her outfit. Everyone expected Reign to rock the same dress in another color when she came down but to their surprise she wore a lose fitting pair of khakis with the same pair of Adidas Unique wore but in blue.

"Sup, yo," she greeted as she came out and turned towards Ogden Avenue. The girls greeted back and fell in step behind her. The weather was nice so they ignored the approaching bus and walked down the hill to the train station.

"Spark up!" Aniqa cheered as soon as they were out of view from the block. Two blunts and one blunt clip came out along with lighters. The teen girls looked like a locomotive as they billowed smoke down the street.

"Hole up, y'all," Reign said when they reached 161st street. She dipped inside Wendy's and ducked into the bathroom. Unique knew exactly what she was doing and wasn't surprised when she emerged in the same dress she wore in blue to match her sneakers.

"OK now!" Treasure laughed. She knew her mother and brother were strict on her. She understood her mom not letting her dress like the rest of them, but not Reef since she sucked his dick quite a few times over the summer.

The girls went upstairs to catch the 4 train and headed to the end of the platform so they could ride in the last car. It was just like the back of the bus where all the action was. Trains ran pretty quickly that time of morning, so they boarded quickly and headed uptown.

All eyes shot towards the platform when they reached the 167th street station since that's the one people from 170th used. They talked loud and ratchet when Leticia and her crew got on. All the catty girls checked each other out while ignoring each other at the same time.

The first day of school has always been and always will be a fashion show. Boys and girls from all corners of the Bronx came to Walton High School dressed to impress. It was too bad they couldn't get graded on their clothes because it would be the only shot some would have to graduate.

Unique was the only one of the crew who really took school seriously. Reign was the leader, but followed her smart friend and paid attention, too. The rest of the girls were there to floss, smoke, fight and flirt.

Fights were a given but rare on the first day of school since that was reserved for flossing. In a week or so, old beefs would be reignited and be back on. The ride back home was as exciting as the ride in. It was more weed and more standoffs on the train. The boys from both blocks snarled at each other while the girls cackled loudly for attention. Both sides wouldn't mind bagging one from the other side but so far only Kidd and Reign had crossed that invisible line.

"Ugly ass bitches," Reign snarled as Leticia and her girls got off at their stop. She squinted and did a double take to verify if she saw who she thought she saw. Leticia her girls, as well as the young boys from the block flocked around the apparition like a returning war vet from Iraq. He was greeted with daps, hugs, and blunts.

"Yo, was that—" Unique also squinted and asked when she saw him, too.

"Nah," she said, shaking her head. The denial didn't stop her from making a beeline over to 170th street as soon as they reached their stop. "We'll catch y'all on the block!"

"Yeah," Unique cosigned as Reign hailed a gypsy cab. Uber will never catch hold in some hood as long as people can catch papi pushing an old school Olds '98 for a couple of bucks. No app needed for that.

"170 and Davidson!" Reign barked and leaned forward for the ride up the hill.

"Thought you said he wasn't going to court 'til October?" Unique asked as they rode up the hill. It was a short walk and even shorter drive and they were half way there before Reign responded.

"That's what he told me," she said and questioned herself. His illegible writing was very hard to decipher, but she was pretty sure that's what he said. He was a cute curly head mixed boy who wrote words the way they sounded to him. His last letter said, "I b hom an oktoba wen I'm go to cort."

They found out soon enough when they reached 170th Street just as the group of teens arrived back on their block. The block was booming as kids from elementary, junior and high school all converged. They spotted who they thought they saw and marched towards them.

"Yo, Reign. Why you don't just call the nigga?" Unique said through clenched teeth.

It was a good idea but too late since they had arrived. Kidd was hugging and rubbing on Leticia's round ass when he looked up and saw her four feet from him.

"What these bitches doing over here?" one of the local girls demanded to know as she began to pounce. Leticia left his side ready to jump in and jump on the intruders. Unique threw her hands up ready to fight, but a word from Kidd cooled their jets.

"Chill," he proclaimed and they chilled. All the eyes on the block shifted in hopes of some excitement since they all knew what Reign didn't. "What you doing here?"

"What you doing here? Thought you ain't go to court until October? Why you ain't call me when you came home?"

"I ain't call cuz I lost my phone when I got bagged," he replied as he steered them towards Ogden and away from the block. "I do go to court in October, but they let me get bond cuz my brother died. Some nigga killed my big brother behind the school the other day."

"Big C, that was your brother?" Reign shrieked and turned pale. Unique balled her face up to signal her to chill.

"Yeah, why? What you heard?" he asked and squinted at her reaction.

"Huh? Oh, nothing. I ain't even get to go to the jam. You know how my moms is," she said, catching her friends warning and adjusting accordingly.

"A'ight, cuz when I find out who kilt my brother, I'ma murder they ass!" he vowed.

Chapter 5

"**O**h girl! He say he gonna kill Reef!" Unique moaned when they reached Ogden and 166th. Neither had spoken or barely breathed until they were off the foreign block.

"No, he not cuz he don't know Reef kilt him," Reign shot back. It took that long to come up with a solution that allowed her to still go with him. He slobbed her down and gripped her booty once he walked them out of eyeshot of the block. 166th and 167th were considered neutral and no one could ask "what you doing over here" or "who you here to see".

"Oh, cuz ain't nobody touching Reef! I'll shoot that whole block up!" she shot back hotly. So hotly, Reign turned and squinted at the love she heard in her voice. Unique's whole face was twisted into a mass of "you bet not touch my man". There was a brief pause while she processed what she just heard.

"Say word?" Reign agreed. Reef had taught them both how to load, cock and shoot on the roof. He also taught them how to fight like a man so they could whoop most girls. She was glad her best friend loved her big brother even though she didn't know her best friend was in love with her big brother.

"So, you still gonna give him some?" Unique wanted to know as much as she wanted to change the subject.

"I'on know," she lied. Her cotton panties were still wet from the kiss they shared a block ago. She felt him get hard when their bodies pressed together while Unique cheered and cheesed from the side. He was definitely getting some pussy first chance they got.

"Ohhh, look it!" Unique warned when they reached 164th Street. As soon as they turned on the block, they saw Rankin's big dread head and gold teeth as he yucked it up with Reef and his right hand man Tito. The mood was festive since the flow of weed was wide open once again.

"Just be easy, ma. He don't know shit," she replied as he turned and locked eyes with her. His spliff blackened lips parted in a smile when he recognized her.

"That's the gal dem," he said and pointed in the girls' direction.

"Who?" Reef asked with a defensive frown when he saw his sister and friend. He wouldn't say it publicly, but he claimed Unique and her tight, wet, hot pussy for himself, and his sister was just that, his sister.

"That's his sister and her friend," Tito chimed in, hoping the dred would catch the warning in his tone.

"Nah, that's not them," Rankin decided even though the wheels were turning in his head. He instinctively reached up and rubbed the spot the bottle opened up. He felt like he had been set up, but a man was stretched out at the morgue, so he let it go for now.

"If you want some broads, I can hook you up," Reef said ready to pass off some of his hand me down pussy. He hit everything on the block and could vouch for most vagina. "Cuz my little sis ain't putting out."

"Rain check," the dred said but checked out Reign's ass as they walked by. If she wasn't putting out then he got played. The thought sent a slow shiver of rage up his spine.

"Mi ah fall true when you ready."

"Bet, won't be but a day or so," Reef replied since the punishment created a back log. He would sell out in a day. Rankin walked away while he was still talking and got in his car.

"Sup with that nigga?" Tito asked since they both caught the change in his demeanor and sudden departure.

"Don't know, don't care. We back in business!" Reef said in a classic half truth. He didn't know, but he did care. He cared more that they were kicking it, smoking and chilling until his sister rounded the corner and the dred went cold. He would put him on Janice and her fat ass and see if that cured what ailed him. If not, he was in danger of getting his head busted again about his sister.

———

"Sup, yo," Kidd drawled all cool from smoking weed and drinking malt liquor all day.

"You," Reign giggled and beamed with pride when he finally called.

"Oh boy," Unique sighed and stood. She shot deuces over her shoulder and headed towards the door. Simone didn't play sleepovers during school nights, so she headed home.

"Just chillin'. My moms in here bugging out over my brother. Tryna plan his funeral and shit," he relayed. Reign paused for a few seconds in search for words. Not to express condolences, but to steer suspicion away from her block and more importantly, her brother.

"Yeah, that's wack, yo. I saw them Jamaicans at the jam. It was a bunch of them ras clot dred locks," she snarled through the lie. She heard the contradiction as soon as it left her mouth, but it was already gone. She could only hope he missed it since he was high and a little slow.

"Thought you said you ain't go to the block party?" he asked, sitting up on his bed.

"Huh? Oh, me and Neek walked through when my moms sent me to the A and P. We ain't stay tho, just passed through. And we saw mad Jamaicans out there! They was deep, yo!"

"Word," he replied and added it to what he heard and knew. His big brother Big C was a notorious jack boy, so it was inevitable that he would one day get gunned down. As sure as Sunday followed Saturday, someone someday would catch him down bad and do him dirty. "Anyway, sup with that pussy? You saved it for me?"

"Yassss," she giggled and squirmed in her seat. She was going to need another shower and change of drawers once he finished talking dirty to her. Meanwhile, Unique heard plenty of dirty talk on the short walk to her building.

"Sup, yo. When you gonna let me put this dick in you, again?" Black asked and gripped his meat through his jeans in case she forgot what dick he was talking about. He made sure to say "again" so his friends knew he hit it once before.

"I would, but you came so quick! I mean like two to three strokes and you was done!" she shot back since he wanted to put people on blast. His dark skin tone prevented everyone from seeing him flushed from embarassment, but he was. She wasn't lying either. It took so much work just to get inside the practically new vagina, he only lasted a few strokes.

"Man, leave that little girl alone," Reef spoke and it became law. The subject was changed to the next chick on her way to the bodega as Unique put a little extra wiggle in her walk since her ass had an audience. Mainly Reef who wished he had time to run up in it tonight, but he had to spend some time with his baby mama and child.

"You ate?" Simone called as soon as she heard her daughter enter the apartment.

"No, you cooked?" she replied and rushed into the kitchen to see what she made.

"Mmhm," she said and nodded, while stirring hamburger

helper. She helped the boxed meal by cutting up onions and peppers into it and made it her own.

"Smells good!" she exclaimed and helped out by making a pitcher of Kool-Aid and grabbing some plates.

"Got weed?" Simone asked as she plated the food. Her part-time job paid what Section 8 and EBT didn't, but she needed sponsors like Bryan for extras like weed and beer.

"Like half a blunt," Unique said, agreeing to share it with her. She had a whole blunt too, but that was for her girl and school. They sat down to eat and chopped it up like friends. "So, what's up with Bryan? He was cute!"

"Bryant," she corrected her like Unique was wrong, then replied, "Yes, he is cute!"

"Ma, that man said his name was Bryan!" Unique laughed. "Just gonna change that man name!"

"Whatever it is, he is something else. A real keeper. I can tell he really likes me!" she rambled hopefully. She stopped just short of bragging on his dick game. Simone may have smoked weed with her child, but that was going too far. She may have been generous with her own vagina, but still tried to instill good morals when it came to her daughter. The last thing she wanted was Unique to follow her footsteps and become a 16-year-old mother.

Unique was hopeful that her mother found a real man. She had witnessed so many come and go, breaking her mother's heart every time. One almost broke her jaw in addition to her heart. What she didn't yet know was some of these grown boys called men were just as bad as the boys her age who just want to hit it and quit it. Fuck a chick, then fuck that chick and move on to the next.

"I hope so, ma. I do," she said then sighed. After they shared a moment, they shared the half blunt which was plenty. Both were happy and high by the time they said their good nights.

———

"Hello, Miss Lopez," Reef said to his baby mama's mother before kissing his baby mama on the cheek and slipping her some cash into her robe. It was both homage and rent for the night.

"How you doing, baby," she said, giving him a firm hug. She always loved when he stopped by to spend time with her daughter and his son. Especially since he always slipped a little cash and weed in her robe.

"I'm good. Hungry," he said when her famous arroz con pollo wafted into his nose. He glanced down at the woman's ass when she spun to fix him a plate.

"You always hungry!" Lisa laughed when she came out holding his son. She popped a kiss on his lips and passed their child off. "I'll fix you plate."

"Bet," he said and sat on the sofa to bond with the baby.

"Well, I'll be in my room," Miss Lopez said and retreated to her room since her daughter took over in the kitchen.

"Hook it up cuz I'm starving!" he called and took a seat on the sofa.

"I got something you can eat, papi," she giggled even though she was serious. She gave him plenty of head, but he was too cool to return the favor. The dudes she dealt with before him all spent time between her thick thighs, drinking straight from the tap.

"You hear yo' moms talking crazy, lil' man?" he said to their baby. The child didn't understand, but laughed anyway since his dad did.

"Mmhmm," she huffed and twisted her lips as she sat his plate before him on the coffee table like a king. She took the baby so he could dig in and get his eat on.

"Yo, ma dukes ain't no joke!" he cheered through a mouthful of food. "I hope she taught you how to make this."

"I ain't got time to be slaving over no damn stove!" she spat.

She made sure to rub his crotch to remind him of where her talents were.

"A'ight, yo," Reef warned as if the rising erection came with consequences. Whatever they were, she wanted it and kept rubbing while he ate. When he neared the end of his plate, she stood and took the baby to her mother.

Lisa didn't do dishes, but she did suck dick. She left his plate on the table and removed his hard dick from his expensive jeans.

"What if your moms come out?" he asked as she inhaled the dick. Her mouth was full, so she shrugged her shoulders and kept going. If she didn't care, he didn't either and leaned back to enjoy the show.

It was a spectacular blow job with lips, tongue and suction working in harmony like a Swiss watch. She put both hands in play, one caressed his balls while the other stroked his shaft. It was no surprise when his legs began to rock while he moaned.

"Mmhm," Lisa hummed and nodded in approval when her man went stiff and busted a nut on her tongue and tonsils. She milked the shaft while swallowing loudly. She had him right where she wanted him. This was the moment to make a wish and it would be granted.

"Dang, ma!" Reef said, looking down as she planted going away kisses on the head of his dick.

"You like that?" she asked needlessly since 99.9% of men like getting their dick sucked. She tucked it away once it deflated in her hand just like it had gotten hard in her hand a few minutes ago.

"Hell yeah," he laughed and retrieved a ready rolled blunt from his pocket.

"We got a problem, baby. That girl seen you wet dude the other night. You know these young broads can't hold water," she suggested.

"Who? My sister? Yo, Reign good, ma," he replied with an exasperated frown on his face.

"Yeah, but what about the other one. Simone's daughter?" Lisa asked.

"Unique cool, too. I practically raised the girl. Her and my sister been friends since they was like 3 or 4."

"Hmph, OK. If you say so," she said with a sigh that said she really wasn't feeling it, but knew there wasn't anything she could do about it. "I hope you right cuz—"

Reef passed her the smoldering blunt to shut her up, but his mind shifted to Unique. He wouldn't admit it out loud, but he wished he was chilling with her instead of here with Lisa. Well, except the head that is. He couldn't help but wonder if the young girl had a head game like his baby mama. Her brand new pussy was tighter, hotter and wetter than Lisa's. An erection jumped in his jeans from thinking about her.

"You ain't even listening to me!" Lisa fussed and snapped him from his daydream.

"I heard what you said," he laughed. "I was just thinking about business and shit."

"Mmhmm," she hummed and twisted her lips. "Anyway, Tito told me they eating good over on Davidson with the blow."

"Good. Let them keep that shit over there!" he fussed since he already knew where she was going with it. What she didn't know is that her cousin Tito was slinging crack on the next block for him. He just refused to let the dangerous drug be sold on his own block. He had a twisted sense of honor that made it okay to sell dope around other peoples' mothers, but not his own. That same twisted sense of honor allowed him to put his dick in his sister's friend, but was ready to kill to keep dicks out his sister.

"I'm just saying, we could be getting all that bread. We can get our own apartment, too! A unit just came open upstairs."

"Man, I'm not leaving my moms and sister! You good right here," he insisted and changed the subject. "Oh, I paid the whip off today!"

"Word? Now we can trade it in for the new one! We pull up with a—"

"Yo, you be bugging! You mad ungrateful!" he shot back, shaking his head. He just paid off a two year old Benz in her name and she talking about a new one. He was smart enough to put it in someone else's name, but dumb enough to use his girl instead of his mother.

"Nah B, I'm just saying. Perez just got a new Benz and Ginger running around talking about how her man the only one getting money in High Bridge," she fussed.

Again Reef saw right through her ulterior motives in an instant. Perez was her ex until he cheated and ultimately chose Ginger over her. He and Reef had always been in friendly competition since they played on the same youth basketball team. Perez went on to lock down the drug trade in the projects while Reef ran his own block. They sometimes did business together, but weren't in competition. That didn't mean their women weren't. Anything one saw the other with had to be one upped. The two kept women were always trying to outdo each other so they could show off in the club and beauty salon.

"Well, you should have stayed with him then," Reef announced and stood to leave. Sometimes a man just wants some head without all the lip.

"Chill, papi," she pleaded and pawed at his zipper. That's how she got him and assumed it was how she would keep him. She failed to realize that every chick on the planet had a pussy and he was starting to prefer Unique's over hers. Her pleas turned to curses once the door closed behind him.

Chapter 6

"Yo, don't think I won't pop up over there!" Sharon warned. She agreed to allow Reign to spend the night at Unique's apartment. That was only after speaking with Simone who assured her she would be home with the girls to ensure no boys would be there.

"Ma, you bugging," Reign said, shaking her head. She knew her mother was bluffing since she had to work, but Simone wouldn't allow any boys in her apartment anyway. Even though she did unknowingly allow her daughter to spend a night with a boy whenever she slept at Reign's.

"I got your bugging!" she shot back, trying to sound hip and failing badly.

"Where, ma? Where you got my bugging?" she teased, looking for it on her body.

"Get off me," Sharon squealed and brushed her daughter off. "I'm just trying to keep you guys safe."

"I know, ma. We good, yo. You raised us right," she assured her. She was right too because she raised her children right despite having to do it by herself. Both Reef and Reign had the same father and he left all three of them when he got sent to prison. Roscoe had too much time to do to do it with a family, so he divorced his wife and turned his back.

"Yeah, I did," she said, accepting the compliment and patting herself on her back. She raised them right even though the streets got a hold of her son. He was just like his father, so she chalked it off as DNA. She just hoped and prayed her daughter picked up her traits and not his. Obviously she didn't hope loud enough or pray hard enough because she was more like her father than Reef.

Sharon walked her daughter over to Unique's building and upstairs to say hello to Simone. Also to look for boys and sniff for weed mainly, but to say hello, too. The woman still turned heads since hard work kept her 41-year-old frame right and tight. Her round ass had more than enough jiggle in her hospital scrubs to turn heads as they made their way. Those same heads would turn away if Reef was out on the block. No one wants a black eye for looking at booty.

"Hey, girl!" Simone sang and rushed over with arms wide when Sharon and Reign walked into her living room.

"How you doing, girl? I...oh," Sharon said when the woman wrapped her into an embrace that made her wonder if they weren't best friends like their daughters. She did take the oppor-tunity to sniff the woman and the air for drugs, but found none.

"Good girl. I see you still working at the hospital. That's good! I'm still at the market," Simone chatted.

"Girl, yes. We be working hard," Sharon said with a little sass to fit in. She spent a few minutes chopping it up before excused herself for work.

"We gone have to hang out one of these days!" Simone suggested as she walked her guest to the door.

"Girl, yes. Just let me know!" Sharon agreed, but Simone was the only one in the room who believed it. The girls twisted their lips and held back giggles at the thought of the hard working stuffy woman going to a club.

Reign went to the window to watch her mother walk up the

block and around the corner to the bus like she always did. And just like she always did, she didn't move until she saw a bus go by.

"Smoke one!" Simone demanded the second Reign turned from the window.

"Word!" Unique cosigned and whipped out a bag of weed. Her mother squinted and moved closer to inspect the colorful herbs.

"Girl, where you get this? All these niggas out there got is old regular weed!" she protested.

"I got my connect," she bragged and popped her collars. Reign recognized it immediately as her brother's personal stash. She was slightly shocked he gave her a whole ounce when he usually pinched her off a few grams.

"My brother gave you that?" she had to ask.

"Your brother gave us this," Unique said when she quickly caught her tone. She was smart enough to avert suspicion even though she hated keeping this secret from her best friend.

"Oh," Reign and let it go. Instead she rolled a blunt while Simone retrieved some wine coolers from her the fridge.

The three girlfriends smoke, drank, danced, giggled and gossiped until Reign's phone rang. She got all giddy and did a little dance before she took the call.

"Sup, Kidd. Mmhm. Yes. OK. I'm on my way," she agreed with a wicked grin.

"You 'bout to go?" Unique asked since she knew where and for what.

"Yes," she said sheepishly and stood. She checked her clothes and hair before heading to the door.

"Let me close my eyes so I can say I didn't see you go nowhere," Simone said. She promised to keep the girls inside, but was easily bribed with weed. She thought it was cute that Reign had a little boyfriend and didn't see any harm in her going downstairs to sit on the steps.

At least that what they told her. She should have known

better since she was 16 when she gave birth to her 16-year-old. Reign slipped out the back way off the block so not as many people would see her. She tensed and walked briskly hoping not to hear her name called. The excitement of her secret mission turned her on even more.

Reign walked in front of the projects on University and took a left down the hill. She let out a big sigh when the motor lodge came into view. It was too late to turn back when she found the room number Kidd gave her and gave it a soft knock. The door was snatched open immediately by a happy Kidd with a smile on his face. He pulled her into the weed smoke-filled room and stuck his tongue in her mouth.

"Nice to see you again, too!" she giggled once the kiss broke off. "How you get a hotel room?"

"I had a junkie rent it for me," he said but didn't say the junkie was his mother. He rented it for her, then rented it from her for a couple hours. "You smoking?"

"Yeah!" she happily agreed even though she was already high as a kite. Reign smoked another blunt, but luckily it was the regular variety as they sipped bitter malt liquor from a 40-ounce bottle. That depleted quickly and it was time to do what she came for. She was here to lose her virginity.

Kidd leaned in and kissed her lips softly to set it off. He groped and pawed her firm, young body until her firm, young breast came out. Reign was introduced to one of her new favorite things when he began to suck her hard nipples. A loud hiss escaped her mouth from the sensational sensation.

The sensual show was paused when he struggled to remove her jeans. Her juices had seeped through her satin panties making a wet spot. They got removed and she covered her face with her arm from shyness. She peeked when he stood and removed his own clothes. She blushed at his pretty penis when it came into view. It was an average six inches with a nice curve to left. It wasn't one of those big dicks all the girls rave about, but she wouldn't know the difference since it was her first. The kissing resumed when he took position between her legs.

"Oww, mph, oww!" Reign complained as Kidd roughly worked himself inside of her. At 17, he had yet to learn the proper way to deflower a virgin or please a woman. Most of the hood rats he fucked had well used, broken in boxes that he could jump up and down in. All she could do was grit her teeth, grip the sheets and take the pain.

"This shit good, yo!" he complimented as he humped. Luckily for her, his inexperience and her super tight, brand new vagina got the best of him pretty quickly. "Shit! Mmmm."

In theory, Reign knew how sex ended, but it took a few seconds to process that he was cumming. Cumming inside of her at that. She suddenly remembered Unique telling how she insisted the couple guys she'd been with use a condom. It was obviously too late now as he grinded away inside of her and filling her up until he was spent.

"I gotta go. Before my moms—" she told him, meaning for him to get up. Her shyness came back when he pulled out of her and stood. It hurt coming out almost as it did going in.

"What? You got your period?" Kidd asked and frowned at the thin coat of blood on his dick.

"No, boy! It was my first time," she admitted sheepishly.

"Say word!" he challenged. She had been telling him she'd never done it before and now he believed her.

"Whatever," she said and got dressed. She winced in pain when she pulled her panties back on her swollen and sore vagina. "What you getting ready to do?"

"Hit the block. Gotta get this money. Plus, I got my ear to the street to find out who killed my brother," he said with a snarl.

"Told you I heard them dreds had something to do with it," she reminded him. He squinted at her to help digest what she was feeding him. She was the only one saying that. Word on the street still pointed to someone from 164th street. Big C was seen talking to a chick before he left and it was slowly coming together.

"Anyway, here," he said and handed her a wad of cash. It looked like a lot more than the hundred bucks it added up to because the twenties and tens were stuffed with ones.

"What's this for?" she asked before taking it.

"You. You my girl, right?" he asked and pressed it into her hand.

"Yes," she blushed and giggled. They dressed and went outside just as his mother hopped out a car. She had more nut in her mouth than a squirrel, so she leaned over and spit the seeds on the asphalt.

"You finished?" she asked with a grimace from the bitter cum she just sucked out some trick's dick. Kidd tossed her the keys in reply and turned away. Reign frowned curiously, but kept her questions to herself. Not that he would have admitted that his mother was a junkie who turned tricks for treats. He certainly wouldn't admit she spent good money with him since he gave her a discount.

"I'll call you tomorrow," he said as Reign got into her taxi. He was back in street mode and forgot about the kiss. He turned and caught the next cab over to his own block.

"Right here, yo," Reign said when the driver reached 165th. She couldn't explain getting out of a taxi if seen since she was supposed to be spending the night at Unique's. She paid the man and went into the bodega, grabbing three wine coolers before walking back around to her block. She got lucky again and didn't get spotted as she went back inside Unique's building and back up to her apartment.

"Sooo?" Unique demanded as soon as she opened the door.

"You gone let me in? Dang!" Reign fussed and giggled. She wanted to tell her all about it, just not out in the hallway. Unique stepped aside so she could enter then locked it behind them.

"Now, tell me all about it!" she shouted in excitement. "Go slow and tell me everything!"

"Where Simone?" she asked since she really didn't want to share her first sexual experience with her friend's mother.

"Girl, her friend Bryan came and took her to the movies. Now tell me!"

"OK, OK. Yo, it was so dope! He was sucking titties and tongue kissing! And he got a big ole dick! I came like four times!" she exaggerated since that's what she heard other girls and women bragging about after sex.

"He did? You did?" Unique frowned curiously. She'd been with four guys and not one made her cum. Reef came close, but came himself just before she got there. So far, sex just hurt.

"Mmhmm," she nodded. "Oh and we smoked some gas! We got blazed and sipped some champagne!"

"Wow," she sighed and lit the next blunt to listen to the lies. She couldn't wait to see Reef again so she could experience what her friend just did. "I know you used a condom?"

"Huh?" she asked not because she didn't hear, but because she didn't use one. She wasn't worried since everyone knows you can't get pregnant on your first time. She still lied and said, "Of course!"

Chapter 7

"**S**up, yo?" Kidd greeted as Woody let him inside his apartment. Actually it was his grandmother's apartment, but she was regulated to her bedroom. Kidd could smell sex and weed in the air of the messy living room. The disheveled hoodrat on the sofa explained both aromas. Hers wasn't the freshest vagina on the block but it was cheap and easy to get.

"Tell him what you told me," Woody demanded as he closed the door behind him.

"Tell him."

"About what?" she asked since she had been talking about everyone and everything since she came over.

"About the jam. At the park. Big C!" he reminded.

"Oh yeah, I seen him at the block party," she said and reached for the blunt in the ashtray. Kidd was all ears since she'd seen his brother the night he died. She wasn't the sharpest tool in the shed either, but no one brought her home for her smarts.

"Who was he with?" Kidd spat hotly.

"With him," she said, pointing at Woody. She linked up with him at the park and came here to smoke and fuck.

51

"We came together, but who you seen him leave the park with?" Woody reminded.

"Oh, that chick Lisa. From 164th. She go with Perez," she said, causing frowns all around.

"Perez? He fuck with us, though," Kidd said. Perez supplied their block since Reef wouldn't. It didn't make sense for him to kill the man.

"Nah, he don't mess with her no more. He fuck with that bad ass chick Ginger from the projects," Woody remembered since Perez had his people check him about trying to talk to her. An unwanted sexual advance will get you sued in Hollywood, but in the Bronx it can get you murdered. Instead of sending speeding slugs his way, he sent his goons to have a word with him. He spared him since he did good business on the block. Plus Ginger was a bad bitch, so he couldn't kill everyone who tried to holla at her. Especially since she wore as little clothes as possible every chance she got.

"Well if she from 164th, that mean one of them 164th Street niggas hit my brother up," Kidd surmised, putting two and two together. Luckily, it was only two plus two because he couldn't count much higher than that.

"Word!" Woody cosigned. He couldn't count very high either, but he would bust his gun. "Yo, you wanna hit this?"

"Nah, I'm good yo. Just smoked one," Kidd declined, assuming he was offering the blunt she just lit.

"Nah, I mean her. Pussy good, yo!" he said like a used car salesman. Remnants of the pussy still lingered in the air causing Kidd to scrunch his face and shake his head.

"Nah, I just hit," he said since he'd just left the hotel with Reign. They gave pounds and he departed back to get his hustle on. He now had a direction to go to avenge his brother's blood.

———

"**M**mhmm," Sharon hummed when Reign returned from her sleepover.

"Good morning to you, too," she replied slightly sharply. She was feeling herself a little now that she was a woman. She had cum-crusted panties in her bag to prove it. The mother squinted at the daughter to decide if she wanted to check her about her tone or not. She knew they would bump heads one day because two women can never live together in perfect harmony. She remembered when she tried her own mother way back when. Her mother put her right on her ass just like she would do to this girl if she tried her.

"Girl, I ain't messing with you today. Been busy as hell all night. Damn kids shooting each other all night," she fussed on her way to her room. It had been an unusually violent night in the usually violent borough of the Bronx. She had been on her feet all night and was ready to get some sleep. She was going to need it since a rash of revenge killings were on tap for last night's death toll.

Reign lifted her chin in victory and went to her own room to finish sleeping. Part of her attitude was having to come home so early to meet her mother. She usually slept 'til noon or beyond on weekends, so she went back to bed.

Reef woke up just before his mom and sister. He had a long night trapping and chasing that bag. Him and Tito spent most of the night on Davidson expanding their crack operations. Weed was good money but peanuts compared to what the cooked coke could bring.

Lisa sucked a shopping trip out of him, so he cut his own sleep short to make good on his promise. His word was his bond, a trait he inherited from his departed dad's DNA. She deserved it too since he could swing through and get sucked off at 1 AM. She was the Burger King of blowjobs. He first took care of home by making lunch for the ladies of his home.

"Mmm, what we got going on out here?" Sharon asked

when she came out her room and was greeted by a wonderful aroma.

"Making lunch for you guys. Where's Reign?" he said, flipping the burgers and frying the fries.

"Probably still sleep," she replied not bothering to hide her disdain. Sharon worked from the time she was 14 to earn her own money. Her own daughter didn't have any hustle or drive. All she wanted to do was dress fly and get high.

Reign heard the voices, then smelled food and got up to investigate both. She refused to learn to cook, so she had to get in where she fit in any time she smelled food. Her vagina still throbbed when she rolled out of bed as a reminder that she was now a woman.

"What's going on out here? Who cooked?" she asked as she bum rushed into the kitchen. Her brother laughed while her mother shook her head as she searched for cooked food.

"Sit down. I got y'all," Reef said and began to plate the food. They did while he put their burgers together the way he knew they liked them.

"You're not eating?" Sharon asked when he served them but not himself.

"Nah, me and Lisa going up to Fordham Road. We gonna eat up there," he explained. Sharon twisted her lips at the mention of the girl's name.

"Oooh, I wanna go!" Reign demanded. She would take a handout anywhere she could get it. Even if it meant being around his stuck up baby mama.

"Bet you do!" Reef laughed and patted her head like a puppy until she knocked it away.

"When you gonna bring my grandson over here?" Sharon fussed. The child lived on the same block, but rarely saw him. Most times she saw the tike in passing and Lisa would barely speak.

"Later," he replied and hoped to change the awkward subject. He knew his mother didn't care for his baby mother.

She claimed the girl had nothing going for herself and dressed like a slut. Reef of course couldn't explain being pussy whipped by that good Puerto Rican pussy.

"Oh and I need to use your car later this week. I wanna go shopping over in Jersey. They got way better food!" Sharon said and went into one of her tirades again about the inferior food in the hood and higher prices. Her kids twisted their lips and snickered at her conspiracy theory, but it was true. The high prices were designed to keep the poor poor while the rich got richer.

"Anytime you want, ma. What's mine is yours," he assured her and sealed it with a kiss on her cheek.

"And mine! When you gone let me drive? I'ma be like—" Reign said and pretended to swerve and drive wild.

"And that's why you won't be driving my shit. Excuse me, ma," he laughed. Sharon had a mouthful of burger and couldn't protest his profanity. "Anyway, I gotta run. Lisa blowing me up now."

"Mmhmm," his mother hummed since she hadn't swallowed. That was the end of her protest and he was out the door.

———

W *ait for it. Wait… for… it*, Leticia thought to herself when Kidd began to moan. His knees bucked and buckled as she sucked him right to the brink and over the cliff.

"Dang, yo!" he marveled and busted a nut on her tongue and tonsils. She was young but had a grown lady head game. He had no idea her step daddy had showed her how to please a man. She clamped down and took it all with loud gulps.

"Can I go with you?" she asked, looking up from her knees. Excellent timing since he could barely breath. She learned from her step daddy that a man is most generous just after busting a nut. Kidd had mentioned going shopping and got his dick sucked as a result.

"Nah, me and Woody going, but here," he said and parted

with a wad of cash. The stack of ones and fives totaled up to $67, but that was plenty. She could buy a pair of cheap sneakers, matching shirt, lunch, weed and still have change left over.

"Bet," she said, accepting the money since she thanked him first. Nothing says "thank you" like swallowing a mouthful of babies. Zeta had spent most of the night with Woody and came up on some cash too, so they were going to Fordham Road.

Kidd departed the staircase and headed down stairs to link up with Woody since he had a car. Meanwhile, Zeta and Leticia hoofed it over to the train for a ride over to the shopping district. The guys honked the horn at them as they flew by. They let them walk even though they both had their semen in their bellies at that moment.

"How much you got?" Zeta asked when they started their journey.

"A lil' something, but I got five on it," Leticia replied. They went half on a sack of weed instead of a cab. At least they were good and high when they reached the D train. The girls gossiped about any and everything and everyone as they rode uptown. Had they been with anyone else, they would have been gossiping about each other, as well. It was just gossip, not personal.

Fordham Road was busy and bustling as usual when they arrived. The first stop was a low budget boutique where hoodrats from all over the borough shopped. They specialized in knock offs and irregulars so low budget broads could dress above their social status.

"Let's get some pizza!" Leticia suggested after they copped some gear. It wasn't a question, so she led her friend towards the pizza shop. Mario's had some of the best slices in the city, so everyone stopped in when they shopped. She spotted a pretty black man and gave a, "Humph! He fine!"

"Yeah, he is!" Zeta said just as loudly so the man's girlfriend could hear. Neither minded starting a fight, so they regularly disrespected chicks.

"Yeah, he is and he got that bag and he got a big dick and —" Lisa fussed and tried to hand the baby off so she could step to the girls.

"Chill," Reef said and held her back. He knew his girl loved to fight and would turn the pizza shop out.

"Hold up, Reef. These nasty lil' bitches got me fucked up," she growled and snarled and got recognized.

"Oooh! Oooh!" Zeta exclaimed when she placed her face. This was the chick who lured Big C from the park. She withdrew and whispered to her friend. "That's that bitch that bruh left with."

"Let's bust her," Leticia said and was ready to step to her on the spot.

"Chill. I'ma tell Woody. Lisa," she said, reading the diamond name plates on her neck and ears. They fell back and let the beef die down. Lisa mean mugged the hoodrats on the way out the shop. She thought she chumped them off since they piped down. She didn't. They just wanted to see what they were riding in.

"They riding good," Leticia had to admit when Reef helped his girl and baby into the Benz. Now they had a car and names to give to Kidd and Woody.

Chapter 8

"**H**mph," Unique said and frowned when her stomach did a whole somersault. The smell of the bacon she was frying suddenly assaulted her whole soul. She tried to fight it but lost and took off to the bathroom. She gripped the bowl and upchucked the entire contents of her stomach. "Whew!"

Unique had tears streaming from her eyes as she stood from the toilet. As soon as she was upright she bent back over and threw up some more. She rinsed her mouth, brushed her teeth and stepped back out the bathroom.

"Girl, I know you ain't burning my food!" Simone fussed as if she bought the bacon with cash instead of an EBT card. She caught it just in time and turned off the flame.

"My bad. My stomach," she said and took over.

"Your stomach what?" Simone challenged aggressively. She looked her daughter up and down like a dare.

"Yeah, right!" Unique huffed when she caught on. "Ain't no babies in here!"

"I notice you ain't say cuz you ain't fucking," she pointed out. She knew her child well enough to recognize what her fluttering eyes meant. It was her telltale sign of nervousness or impending lies. It was clear her child was now having sex and once they start they don't stop. Who would know better than she. "Girl, I hope you smart enough to use protection!"

"Yes, mommy," she admitted sheepishly. It was partially true since the couple guys she slept with before Reef used condoms. He never did and almost always pushed in instead of pulling out. That of course made her think of her missing her period. It wasn't late. It was gone and it suddenly explained the other symptoms she learned in health class. She planned to boost a pregnancy test later even though she was certain at that second she was pregnant. If there was one caveat it was her being 100% certain who the father was. Unlike her mother who had more possible candidates than a bad spades hand.

"What?" Simone shrieked as she watched the wheels turn in her daughter's head.

"Nothing, mommy! You buggin', yo!" she shot back with way more attitude than her mother would stand for.

"You buggin talking to me like one of them bitches on the street! I guarantee you can't whoop my ass," Simone vowed. She even crossed her heart and stressed, "On God, this ain't want you want!"

"Nah, I don't want no smoke, ma," she surrendered. She still left a little spunk in her tone to prove she wasn't no punk. Simone heard it and appreciated it because she did not and would not raise a punk.

"You got weed?" Simone asked now as they had an understanding. Bryan hadn't come by in a week, so she was tapped out of cash.

"No. I'm holla at Reign's brother later, tho," she said. She left out the part about being pretty sure she was pregnant by the man.

"With his fine ass!" he mother cheered which was slightly creepy to Unique since she was sleeping with him.

"Ma!" Unique cried out in utter embarrassment. Her mother frowned curiously and made an educated guess.

"Oooh, you messing with him? Girl, that's why you be spending the night over there!" she ascertained. It wasn't a wild guess since she lost her own virginty at a sleepover. A friend's cousin got that cherry when everyone else went to sleep.

"No!" she shouted, causing her mother to twist her lips dubiously.

"Mmhmm," Simone huffed and let it go. Her daughter was fucking now and ain't no stopping that once it starts.

————

"S up with you?" Reign frowned when Unique met up with the crew for the trek to school. The faraway gaze in her eyes said something was up.

"I'm good, yo," she replied, giving the other girls a glance that her friend understood to mean it was private. She gave a nod that said "we'll talk later" and she left it alone.

"Fire this up," she directed and handed over a blunt. The girls stomped down to the train station and headed to school.

There was the usual tension when Leticia and her crew boarded, but no lines were crossed, so no blows were exchanged. Leticia and Zeta had filled the girls in on Lisa and Reef a couple weeks ago. Kidd and Woody were watching and waiting for a chance to strike. He and Reign linked up twice more to repeat their first sexual episode.

After an uneventful school day, the girls headed back home. No one learned a lick today including Unique who was deep in thought most of the day. Her girls mainly flirted and played like any other day.

"Y'all go 'head. We got a stop to make," Unique said when the train let them out at 161st Street. Neta became the leader anytime Reign and Unique weren't around, so she led the journey up the hill to their block.

"What you got, yo?" Reign asked as Unique led her into the grocery store. She knew something was up since they didn't stop at the one Unique's mother worked at and got a huge discount since the woman wouldn't scan most of their items. There were steaks and shrimp in the fridge right now from the hook up.

Unique explained her dilemma by concealing a pregnancy test under her hoodie. Reign never liked to be left out, so she stole one, too. It didn't register until they walked by the register on the way out. Both girls held their breath in case the items sounded an alarm or cameras had spotted them. In either event, they would have taken off on foot and ran home.

"Yo, why we boosting pregnancy tests?" Reign asked as they walked briskly away from the supermarket. Unique didn't reply, so she had to figure it out on her own.

"I'on know," she shrugged and kept walking. "My shit ain't come and I threw up this morning."

"Dang! So whose is it? Charles, Black? I hope it ain't Tito's old ass! I'on even know why you gave him some!" she grimaced. Tito was a handsome, black Puerto Rican and was getting plenty of paper, but already had five kids in High Bridge already. He was 23, which was quite old to a 16-year-old.

"I'on mess with none of them no more!" Unique shot back indignantly. Now it was Reign's turn to frown when she wondered who else it could have been.

The two were inseparable, so there was no way she had some secret boyfriend. Her frown deepened when she decided it had to been Simone's new man. Bryan had looked her up and down, concentrating on her crotch and breast when she came over. She twisted her lips to keep them closed and accepted her findings.

Unique decided to stay tight lipped until one, she took the test and two, told the baby father first. Her chin lifted on its own when she decided she was keeping it, no matter what. If Reef got mad, she would just handle it on her own. She figured if her mom could raise a child on her own than she could, too. She could, but it ain't easy.

"A'ight, yo. Just umm, get at me," Reign said as they reached her building. She would tag along while she took the test if she was invited, but she wasn't.

"Yeah," Unique said and pressed on. Simone was leaving for work when she reached her building.

"Sup, yo. Here, buy a hero," her mother said, giving her daughter money for dinner.

"K, thanks," she said sadly and detoured to the bodega. Her heart smiled before her face when she saw Reef at the counter paying for his purchases.

"Sup, yo. Hey, take whatever she getting out of that," he told the clerk about the twenty he just handed him.

"Hey. Turkey and cheese. Oh, and a juice and chips!" she said, rushing around to gather her dinner. Reef locked in on her butt cheeks, watching them wiggle while she walked.

"Yo' your moms home?" he asked when she returned to the register. The look in his eyes explained the other questions he had.

"No," she said, blushing and batting her eyes. "You coming up?"

"Yeah. Give me a few," he said not saying a few what. It could have been a few minutes or a few hours, but he passed her a blunt to hold her over until he got there.

Unique was still blushing and moist between her legs when she reached her empty apartment. She had almost forgotten about the pregnancy test until she remembered she had to pee.

"Oh yeah!" she said and scrambled to get the strip under the stream of pee already in progress. She made it and sat it aside to wipe and wash her hands. She decided to eat since she had to wait for the results. After she devoured half the sandwich and juice, she lit up the blunt. One toke confirmed it was his private stash and not the bullshit they sold on the block. A few turned out to mean an hour because Reef was ringing her bell.

"Hey," she said as she opened the door. He rushed his tongue into her opened mouth and twirled it around. They kissed over to the sofa and fell down on it.

"Do me a favor," he said as he leaned back and withdrew his erection. Unique was about to ask what kind of favor, but he was already directing her head towards his pretty dick. She opened her mouth to agree and he slipped inside of it. It was "yes" in sign language.

Unique wasn't sure how to do it, but he helped by moving her head and thrusting his hips. He knew it was her first time and that turned him on even more. Her virgin mouth was just as hot and tight as her young pussy. It was nowhere near the spectacular blowjobs Lisa was famous for, but still got the job done.

"Shit!" he exclaimed and exploded in her mouth. The firm grip on her head prevented her from running.

"Humph!" she fussed as her mouth filled with salty semen. She was both disgusted and fascinated at the same time. She wouldn't swallow, so cum escaped the corners of her mouth and onto his jeans.

"Dang, ma!" he cheered at the sensation. Nevermind the jeans because he had plenty.

Unique popped up and took off down the hall to the bathroom. She spit what was left into the toilet, then rinsed her mouth vigorously. Once she finished that, she brushed twice while Reef giggled about it in the next room. Unique spit toothpaste into the toilet once more and noticed the pregnancy test. She let out a deep sigh and picked it up. She carried it back into the living room and found Reef naked on the sofa. That was a good appetizer, but he was ready for the main course.

"What are you doing?" she laughed, seeing him taking even his socks off. The sight was so sexy and amusing, she forgot about the positive plus sign on the strip.

"About to fuck the shit out of you!" he vowed and began to help her out of her clothes. His mind had been on the young girl all day after a night with his irritating baby mama. He had her naked except for the test strip in her hand. "What's that?"

"Huh? Oh! Oh yeah, here," she said passing it forward. "I'm pregnant."

"By me? You ain't been with none of these niggas on the block, have you?" he asked even though he was sure she hadn't. Dudes are very much like woman and he would have heard some gossip if someone else hit.

"No!" she reeled, repulsed at the thought of anyone but him ever touching her.

"Good! You keeping it, too!" he insisted and laid her down. Unique thought she was in trouble when he lifted one of her legs up on to the back of the sofa. She walked out on Bryan and her mother fucking like that a few nights ago and it looked painful. Instead Reef kissed her plump thighs and touched her vagina.

"Ssss," she hissed when he leaned in and licked her. It was a first for him too, but eating pussy is pretty much self explanatory. He used her moans and wiggles as a road map and made her cum all over his mouth.

She hissed again when he popped up from her pussy and plunged inside. She found out she was right about that position being painful as he began to pound.

"My bad," he said gently when he realized he was hurting her. He let her leg down and stuck his tongue back in her mouth. Unique felt electric currents flowing through her body as he made love to her.

"I... feel," she said, pausing then moaned when a crazy feeling engulfed her. She could live to be 120 and never cum as hard as she came that first time on her sofa. Tears streamed from her eyes as her whole body shook the whole sofa. She shook so hard she shook another nut out of Reef.

Chapter 9

"Oh my God! Your car rides so smooth!" Sharon proclaimed when she returned from her shopping trip. She called ahead so her son could unload the trunk full of groceries. She almost called him earlier when some goons pulled up next to her as she passed over 170th Street. She thought they were about to try to carjack her. They pulled along side and the passenger took a good look at her and shook his head. She could still see the malice in his eyes when she looked in them. A shiver ran up her spine from the memory.

"I'ma buy you one," Reef vowed as he collected the bags. Tito came over to help out as well.

"I don't know," she said wearily. She felt a contradiction between her disdain of drug money and the smooth ride. The smooth ride won out and she smiled, "OK, blue please."

"Blue, it is!" he agreed. He'd rather buy a whole 'nother car than go through another argument with Lisa about the car.

She had a fit when he let his mother use the vehicle since it was in her name. Truth was she was just jealous over any and every other female in his life. He made up his mind to switch the car to his name before he cut her off because he was definitely about to cut her off. She could go back to Perez since she was so worried about what he was driving and wearing.

"Uh oh! We 'bout to smash!" Reign cheered when she saw the groceries coming into her apartment. She twisted her lips when she saw Tito bringing up the rear. He smiled and shot a glance at her crotch area. That's the main reason he offered to help out anyway.

"Appreciate it. I'll be down in a minute," Reef said, dismissing his friend. He didn't like men around his mother and sister and hadn't had friends over since he was 12. That was around the time he started noticing how fine some of his friends' mothers were and didn't want anyone looking at his like that.

"A'ight, yo," he agreed and stole another glance at Reign and a peek at Sharon's round ass on his way out.

"About to make me a sandwich," Reef said and put his phone on the counter and dug in.

"Make me one, too!" Reign pleaded like the spoiled baby sister. "I want turkey and ham!"

"One or the other! I don't get no stamps, you know!" Sharon fussed. A lot of people she knew who got EBT cards often splurged on meals since it was free.

"Turkey then," Reign pouted and almost got popped. The unnecessary attitude inched the mother and daughter an inch closer to the inevitable butting of heads.

"Alright, alright!" Reef said as his phone buzzed on the counter. It sounded like cold hard cash, so he rushed to make the sandwiches. He was in such a rush to get that money, he rushed out without his phone.

"My bad, yo," Tito apologized unapologetically for blowing his phone up when Reef emerged from the building. "We need to shoot up to 181st and get this dough."

"Bet," he agreed and headed to his car. They got in and pulled off the block. A left on Ogden got them pointed uptown to where a decent sale waited on them.

"See, if you put me onto the connect I coulda made the run and been done," Tito reminded him. He tried to get the connect at least once a day.

"Who, Rankin?" he laughed. He didn't mind him taking over the weed business because the coke was booming. He laughed even louder when he saw the sour look on his friend's face. He was laughing so hard he didn't see the Jetta pull out behind them as they crossed 170th Street.

"Man, that weed is cool, but we getting the check up over on Davidson. We should set up shop on the block. Like at the end of the street so junkies don't gotta come two blocks to cop," Tito said. Reef looked at him out of the corner of his eye. Dude suggested a different scenario every day to move the deadly drug to the block.

"Son, them fiends would walk to the moon for a blast!" he shot back.

"True but niggas be short stopping them. They might cop something before they get to us and we missing out!"

"Bruh, we getting rich. We ain't missing shit. What you owe me now? It's time to re-up," he said and reached for his phone. He kept a ledger of every coin owed to him on the SD card. It was then he realized he left it. "Shit!"

"Sup, yo?" he asked in reply to the outburst. Reef turned to reply just as the Jetta whipped around and pulled along side of them. He saw the danger but it was too late.

"This for my brother!" Kidd shouted and shot. He let four rounds go through the open window, but only needed one. Reef slumped over the wheel dead on arrival from a shot to his temple. Tito ducked out the way and lived.

"Oh shit! Oh shit!" Tito shouted and grabbed the wheel to prevent the car from sideswiping parked cars.

He pulled the emergency brake up and brought the car to a stop in the middle of the street. He jumped out and took off towards the block as the Jetta sped off. He hated to leave his partner like that, but hated going to jail even more. Jail would be exactly where he was going if he waited around in a car full of dope and a gun under the seat. He grabbed the drugs from inside the car, but there was no time to empty the trunk.

———

"You must have got this from my brother?" Reign said when she hit the blunt. She decided to go over to chill during the small window of time between Simone coming from work and Sharon leaving for work. The knock on the door had awoken Unique from her dick-induced nap.

"Yeah," she sighed, meaning that wasn't the only thing she got from her brother. She had a baby in her belly and a box full of cum right now from her brother. Now she had to figure out how to break it to her. Being absentminded helped break the news since the positive test was still on the table. Luckily, Reign did come before her mother did because she had to break the news to her, as well.

"I see you pregnant, huh? What you gone do?" she said between tokes. She passed her the blunt despite the revelation. Every chick they knew on the block who had a baby smoked while carrying it, so it was no biggie.

"I'ma keep it. You gonna be an auntie again," she said and took a pull.

"I already know! I see! I hope it's a boy! We gone have his ass fly as hell!" she cheered since motherhood in the hood was a baby fashion show. A lot of kids didn't have cribs or walkers, but had Jordans and designer clothes.

"I'm saying, yo. You gonna be an aunt, like blood relative," Unique said again.

"I know! We family!" she shot back and hugged her best friend. Her demeanor changed to somber when she remembered her assumption that it was her mother's boyfriend impregnated her. "It is Bryant, right?"

"Bryan? What?" she asked and frowned up perplexed. "You think? Eww! No!"

"My bad!" Reign said and laughed at the look of pure disgust on her friend's face.

"Yeah, that would be nasty fucking behind yo' moms. So, who the daddy then?"

"Told you twice already. You gonna be aunt again," she said and watched the wheels turn. Reign's face switched from curiosity to confusion then flashed with anger.

"Yo, tell me you not pregnant by my brother. *Tell me you not pregnant by my brother!*" she demanded, punctuating each word with a palm punch. Unique shrugged her shoulders because she couldn't tell her that. She could, but it would be a lie.

The slap that followed surprised both girls. They stood there for several seconds trying to figure out what happened. Unique reached to her stinging cheek and figured she'd been slapped. Reign caught on by her stinging hand, but neither remembered the actual slap. She didn't mean to, but she wasn't exactly sorry either. She turned and stormed out of the apartment and marched home.

The block was buzzing as word of a murder up the avenue trickled back. Tito detoured to the projects, so word hadn't reached them that one of their own was slumped behind the steering wheel. Reign was red from rage and missed most of the chatter as she stomped back home. To make matters worse, her constant calls to her brother went unanswered. She planned to give him a slap too when she caught up with him.

"Girl, what's wrong with you? Barging in and slamming my door!" Sharon shouted. She shouted some more when the girl ignored her and slammed her room door. She was already hot from her son's phone ringing nonstop on the counter. "Damn kids."

Sharon showered and went back into her room to dress for work. She noticed her sexy frame in the full length mirror. A smile spread on her face when she saw she still had it, then slipped into her scrubs for work. She matched her sneakers with her clothing and stepped from her room. The thought to check on her child crossed her mind, but she wasn't in the mood for her.

"I'm gone!" she called as she hit the door. She wanted to turn to see if her little girl was watching from the window but wouldn't know how to take it if she wasn't. A needless worry since Reign was right there as usual. Her face was twisted up but she still watched her mother walk down the block and around the corner. She stood there until the bus pulled off and barreled down the block. Almost an hour later she arrived at her job.

"Hey girl!" Sharon's coworker called when she entered the emergency room for work. The troubled look on her face made her asked, "What's wrong?"

"Huh? Nothing, I'm fine," she said even though she had a nagging sense of dread that she couldn't explain. It didn't make any sense so she shrugged it off. "What we got going on?"

"Girl, some poor man got shot on Ogden. The body on the way now so doc can pronounce him," she said. She went on to explain the rest of the goings on in the popping E.R. Sharon got in where she fit in and began to tend to patients.

"DOA incoming," a EMT driver announced as he wheeled a gurney in.

They took him to a bay so the attending doctor could sign off on it so it can go down to the morgue. Sharon just shot a curious glance at the passing stretcher. She did a double take at the expensive sneaker peeking out the bottom of the bloody blanket. Her and Reef had a lengthy debate on the merits of $250 basketball sneakers, especially for a man who didn't play the sport anymore.

He explained that he was still a baller even off the court. It was the conversation that made her press forward. She couldn't live with the coincidence and pressed forward. She needed a peek just to verify that this wasn't her child. She followed the

EMTs into the bay for a look. She lifted the sheet and that's a fucked up way to find out your son was dead.

———

"Sup, yo. Meet me at the spot," Kidd asked as soon as Reign picked up. He was amped up about the murder and hoped to visit her vagina. She knew he meant the same motel they met at twice before.

"You know I can't go nowhere during the week," she shot back and felt a throb in her vagina at the thought. They'd linked up the last few weekends when she spent the night with Unique. It looked like those days were dead because she vowed to never speak to her ever again.

"Yeah, OK," he said quickly since he did know the answer. He had plenty of pussy on his own block so he cut the call short. "I'll call you later tonight."

"OK, I—" she began, but he was gone before she could finished.

She shrugged and took a pull off her blunt. The door opened and she waited for her brother to come in so she could flip on him, too. Instead her mother walked in looking like she was in shock. She scrambled to put out the weed, but that wouldn't do anything about all the smoke in the air. "My bad, ma!"

"It's OK," she sighed and plopped down next to her.

They both sat in silence trying to process their next words. Reign needed to explain how the house got full of weed smoke since she was forbidden to smoke in the house. Her mother gave up on the futility of telling her she couldn't smoke, so she demanded she not do it in her apartment.

Meanwhile, Sharon was trying to find words to break the nasty news of her brother's death. The look of shock and sorrow pasted on Reef's face when she lifted the sheet would forever haunt her. She attempted to stay at work because she

71

really couldn't afford a day off. Especially now that her son's supplemental income died with him.

Sharon reached over and took her baby girl into her arms and held as tightly as she could. Reign initially flinched from the sudden movement until she realized she wanted to hug, not fight. They sat there rocking for several minutes before someone spoke.

"Reef's dead," her mother quietly said.

"What you say?" Reign asked and pulled away so she could look at her mother. The anguish in her eyes told her she had heard correctly but she still insisted, "What you just said!"

"He's gone. Reefy is dead," she sighed desperately. She needed consoling herself, so there wasn't much she could do for her daughter. Her wails combined with hers, but they were on their own. They screamed and moaned together, but separately. Reign eventually reached for the blunt and lit it back up. She half expected her mother to say something and she did. Reign blew a smoke ring towards the ceiling.

"Huh?" she asked instead of the "excuse me" her mother usually insisted upon.

"I said let me hit that," Sharon repeated. Reign watched as she took the blunt and took a deep pull. She let some of the smoke billow out of her nose and inhaled into her nostrils. She was impressed, but she didn't know her mother and father conceived her after smoking a blunt.

The two rocked and smoked while the news began to circulate around the block. Lisa decided to put on a big show and take her show out on the street. She put on, wailing and ranting about revenge and conspiracies. No one got the official report since Tito was laid up in the projects. He was still shook up from the sudden act of violence to speak about it.

"Pssh," Unique huffed when Neta called again. She just knew Reign ran and told everyone who would listen how she forced her brother to fuck her. How she held a gun to his head and took the dick.

Simone took a call on her own phone and got the news. She rushed into her daughter's room to be first to spread the news.

"Yo! You heard about Reef?" she shouted. Unique was now really hot at Reign for snitching to her mother before she got to tell her herself.

"I was going to tell you ma. I'm—"

"I know you are baby. He was a good dude," she said sadly. Unique frowned at cocked her head curiously.

"What you talking about, ma?" she demanded.

"He dead. Reef got killed up the street!"

Chapter 10

"**S**up, Kidd. What you doing?" Reign sighed when Kidd took her call. He looked down at Leticia's yellow naked body and lied.

"Nothing," he said since it beat the truth. The hoodrat was sound asleep in his bed from a long night of smoking and fucking. Reign wished she had her best friend to grieve with but Unique violated. She just knew she seduced her brother against his will. She spent most of the night trying to crack the code on his phone but had no luck. He had to change it quite often because Lisa was a real code breaker and kept getting inside. "Sup with you? You sound funny?"

"My brother got killed on Ogden yesterday," she said and began crying once more.

"Word! Wait! What?" he said when her words registered. "In the Benz? That was your brother?"

"Yeah, Reef. You heard about it?" she asked and sat up. Leticia stirred awake from his outburst so he stepped into the next room to continue.

"Yeah, I did. It was a few blocks up," he said, while the wheels turned in his head. He wasn't the sharpest knife in the drawer, but sensed something wasn't right. "Come over here. I wanna see you."

"To your block?" she asked and frowned. It wasn't cool to hang out over there with their hood/rats mean mugging and slick dissing, especially without her main chick by her side. Still she was in love and mourning, so she agreed. "OK. Let me get dressed."

Reign was so excited she hung up without saying goodbye. She had already showered but took another one and got dressed. Her mother was shut in behind her door and didn't see the sexy outfit she selected. She eased out the door and down the steps.

She refused to look down the block towards Unique's building, so she wouldn't have to see her. She avoided all the long faces as she marched over to Ogden Avenue and hailed a gypsy cab. Tears escaped her eyes as she rode up the few blocks looking for comfort in her boyfriend's arms.

"Right here," she told the driver when she saw Kidd standing in front of the bodega. She paid papi and hopped out the car. She rushed towards him wearing a smile, but was the only one. Kidd had an angry scowl on his face when she reached him. She was the one in mourning, but still asked, "What's wrong with you?"

"Yo, first you said you ain't go to the block party, then you said you did. And mad people saw you there! Then you the only one talking 'bout some dreds hit my brother up. Bitch, you knew yo' brother did that shit!" he yelled. It also explained why Leticia and a pack of rats suddenly rushed out of the bodega.

Reign realized she was about to get jumped but didn't try to run or plead. Reef taught her how to fight, not run so she swung on the closest girl to her. Leticia was the unlucky volunteer who got socked. The haymaker knocked a tooth out her mouth but it would be her only lick. The girls pummeled her down to the ground while Kidd watched.

"Beat that bitch the fuck up," Kidd directed and they acted.

Reign balled up to deflect the blows, but there were too many punches and kicks. Someone hit her with a bottle that stretched her out. She was roughly a minute or so from being beaten to death when a stray patrol car happened by.

"Five-O!" a lookout called like he was paid to do. Each girl got in a last stomp or kick before taking off. They scattered in different directions, leaving her unconscious on the concrete.

"She OK?" a cop called to Kidd who still stood nearby. He just shrugged and kept watching.

"I'll call a bus," the other cop said and called an ambulance. They waited until one arrived and put Reign in the back. She woke up just before the doors closed and saw Kidd wearing a satisfied smirk on his now ugly face. He was now the ugliest person she'd ever seen in her life. She wanted to have her big brother beat him up, but didn't have one anymore. She wanted to get her best friend so they could get some get back but didn't have one those anymore either.

———

"**M**rs. Brown?" a voice asked when Sharon finally answered the phone. It had been ringing for quite a while and her calls for Reign to pick it up went unanswered. She had no idea her daughter had left the apartment.

"Miss," she corrected even though she never changed her name back after her divorce. The number on the screen finally registered and she realized it was her place of employment. "This is Nurse Sharon Brown, E.R. Who is this!"

"I'm sorry, Sharon. I thought that was Reign, but I wasn't sure!" her coworker replied. She had met both her kids several times over the years but couldn't believe the lumped up woman in the emergency room was the same girl. She was able to give a name and number before passing out once more.

"Reign? What about her!" she reeled.

"You need to get down here. She got jumped. I—hello?" she said, but Sharon was already out the front door.

"Hey, Unique! Come with me!" she demanded when she saw her daughter's friend coming out of the store.

"Hey, Miss Sharon," she greeted with her head down. She couldn't look her in her face from her own grief and guilt of being pregnant by her son. She didn't know if Reign had told her or not, but she still hadn't told her own mother. "Me and Reign not—"

"She's in the hospital! Someone jumped her!" she said and pulled the girl by her arm. Unique gave up her protest and went along with the woman. She had just lost her son and now her daughter was in the hospital. Not the time to tell her they were beefing, especially since she would ask about what.

Sharon could hardly afford to take a taxi, but since she didn't know the condition of her child, she couldn't afford not to. They rode in silence all the way to the hospital and rushed inside.

"She in triage," a nurse told her and led the way. Sharon was used to seeing the violent results of the violent city but it was different when she saw her daughter.

Reign's head looked twice as large and both eyes were swollen shut. Her lips were cut and her pretty skin was black and blue. *No wonder the nurse didn't recognize my baby,* she thought to herself.

"Who did this to her?" Unique heard herself ask.

"She was found unconscious on 170th Street," the nurse replied and Unique took off out the door. Sharon was so busy tending to her new patient, she didn't see her leave.

"Any fractures?" she asked and double checked her vitals.

"No. Probable concussion," the nurse replied and filled her in on what was done and what was to come. Meanwhile Unique was outside hailing a taxi.

"170th and Nelson Ave!" she ordered so forcefully the driver

77

turned and frowned. "Aye, yo! You ain't the only cab out here. You gone drive or what?"

The driver responded by driving since that's what drivers do. Unique was so hot about seeing her friend fucked up, she rocked back and forth and punched her palm as they rode up the hill. The meter was close to the twenty bucks she had when they reached her destination. She pressed her last bill through the partition and he hit the locks that locked her in. Leticia and the pack of rats were still in front of the store, so she made a beeline towards them.

"Yo, which one of you bum bitches touched my friend? You? You? Huh?" she asked getting in all their faces. The girls all flinched assuming she had a gun. This was the Bronx after all and chicks bust their guns, too. Just ask Remy Ma.

"Yo, this bitch is crazy!" Zeta announced when no gun came out. The mood changed in a New York minute once they realized she was unarmed.

"Yeah, I'm crazy!"

Unique shouted and proved it by swinging on her. She went in for almost a minute until being overcome by all the fists and feet.

"Y'all bitches chill! We don't need Five-O back out here again!" a dope boy demanded. They lost money when patrol cars patrolled after Reign got beat down. The warning came too late because Unique lay sleeping in the same spot as her friend. An ambulance was called to take her away, too.

———

"Looks like we got another one" a nurse sighed when another ambulance arrived with another beat up girl. This one wasn't as beat up as the last one, but beat up nonetheless. Hearing the call came from the same block caught Sharon's attention. Reign was battered, but would make a full recovery. She already sent a coworker for cocoa butter to help heal the bruises. She stole a second away to see who this new patient was since they came from the same place her child was hurt. If it was one of the girls who hurt her they came to the wrong hospital because they were about to get worse, not better.

"Unique! Girl what the hell!" she exclaimed seeing who the patient was.

"They fight my sister they gotta fight me, too!" she declared. She recited it just like Sharon had taught them since they first became friends. She made them vow to always look after each other. As a result, they beat up and got beat up. But they did it together.

"Yeah, well" Sharon said proudly. "But now I gotta call your mother."

"Do you have to?" she complained even though she knew she had to. She did and an hour later Simone rushed in raising hell.

"Where's my baby! How's my baby? Oh my baby!" she fussed until she was by her side. She went from worry to warrior the second she saw her battered baby. "Who did this to you?"

"Just some random chicks. Hating cuz I'm fly," she said since she knew her mother would rush up to 170th Street, too. Simone was a little tougher than them and some of those girls would have been coming to the hospital with her. A doctor arrived with her chart to fill the parent in so she could go home.

"No fractures or concussion. A few bumps and bruises but she and baby are just fine. No sign of miscarriage," he read.

"Ok, thank you," Simone sang and began to sign the paperwork. She was almost done when the words all registered. "Wait, miscarriage? What you mean miscarriage? What he mean miscarriage?"

The doctor raised his hands and backed out of the room. Not a day went by that he didn't see a pregnant teen. He was immune to it and left Unique to explain for herself.

"I'm pregnant" she said since that summed it up.

"What! Girl how could you do this to me! I aint tryna be no

32-year-old grandmother. I ain't about to stop going to the club to watch your kid!" Simone shrieked. She fussed all the way home.

———

"Can you bring me my phone, too? I left it at home," Reign guessed. Guessed wrong because it was taken when she got jumped. The girls couldn't get in it so they smashed it on the sidewalk.

"OK, baby," she agreed but knew it would take a while on the bus since she couldn't afford another taxi.

"Want me to drive you?" her coworker asked.

"Would you? Thank you!" she agreed and off they went. The woman made small talk as they rode over to High Bridge. Sharon saw her friend grimace when they reached her block. She wasn't ashamed but still explained, "It's all I can afford."

"I'm sorry, girl. I grew up in the projects, so I know," she explained. What she didn't explain was living in a loveless marriage just so she could afford to keep her own children out neighborhoods like this.

"Yeah, well after losing my son and almost losing my daughter in one week I gotta get out of here. I gotta get out of here!" she almost pleaded. It was as close to breaking down as she came since her husband left. She tried to stay strong, but was nearing the end of her rope. She let out a sigh and sucked it up for now.

Sharon rushed upstairs and put on some soup then looked for her daughter's phone. She and Reef had the same model phone but Reign kept a pretty pink case on hers. The one she found in her room didn't have a case so she assumed she took it off. She looked for the charger and found it, but found the pregnancy test she boosted along with it. She didn't know her daughter boosted it just because her friend did. She often asked Reign if Unique jumped off a cliff would she jump too. She always said no, but truth be told, she would. She would certainly jump right off the cliff with her.

"Man," Sharon moaned and her knees buckled from the weight of the pregnancy test. It was unopened but its presence said her child was now fucking and maybe pregnant. The weight on her shoulders just got heavier. The end of her rope just got nearer.

"You OK?" her coworker asked when she returned looking like she was in shock. She saw the change in the changed woman.

"Huh? Uh, yeah. I'm fine," she said, but she wasn't fine. She was as far from fine as one could be.

Chapter 11

"Thank you, mommy," Reign sang when her mother returned with her food and more importantly her phone. She was plenty hungry but also thirsty to see what the streets were saying.

"Yeah, you're welcome," she said stoically as she entered. She saw the nurse removing the bed pan and sprang into action.

"I got it! I got it. I don't mi—" the nurse said, but Sharon snatched it away.

"I said I got it!" she said.

The fresh pee inside sloshed, but didn't spill. They both looked down to make sure they didn't get splashed. Nursing is a hard enough job without getting pee on you. The nurse screwed her face up at the close call, but Sharon spoke up before she did.

"My bad. It's been a rough week."

"I know, honey," she said and gave a half hug since she had a full pan of pee.

She was happy the boss put Sharon on the clock so she could keep getting paid. She got paid to take care of her own kid. Kinda like a housewife, but without a husband. Sharon took the pan into the bathroom and ran it over the test strip.

She sat the test on the counter and went back out to Reign. Reign quickly realized this wasn't her phone, then recalled taking her phone with her to 170th Street. She shook her head knowing she would never see it again. She would just keep Reef's since he wouldn't need it anymore.

"What, baby? Too hot? Too cold?" Sharon asked, assuming the head shake was due to the soup.

"Nah, ma. My brother," she said and pouted. Reign spooned soup into her mouth with tears streaming down her face.

Sharon let out a frustrated sigh when she looked at her watching the time before she went to check the pregnancy test. She stood and entered the bathroom. She looked at the results and stuck the strip into her pocket and walked out.

"What's wrong, ma? Where you going, mommy?" Reign asked as Sharon walked through the room and out the door. She couldn't deal with her pregnant daughter at the moment and went to have a drink. There was a bar nearby she passed going to and from work. She often looked over at it but never ventured inside. Not until today that is as she went in and ordered a Seven and Seven like her man used to drink. Meanwhile, Reign went back to trying to break into her brother's phone.

"Um, Sharon?" she guessed and typed. It was another incorrect password, so she tried again. She tried her own name, their father Roscoe, his son Rinaldo, but nothing worked. She did know he frequently changed it to keep Lisa out, so on a whim she tried Unique's name.

"Wow!" she exclaimed when her ex best friend's name opened the phone. She wanted to blame Unique for breaking into the phone and changing the password to her name, but that just didn't make any damn sense. The phone buzzed and chirped for a few minutes from incoming messages. Last minute goodbyes from people all over the city. Tears streamed down her face seeing how many people loved her brother.

Reign knew the 'Neek' in his contacts was Unique and went

to be nosey. She ended it with an eye full of his dick and her pussy since they traded pics daily before he died.

"Nasty ass," she fussed like she didn't have any dick in her phone.

The sexually charged messages showed they were really into each other. She moved on to the phones gallery and found more pussy. Lots and lots of pussy in all shapes, colors and sizes. She saw a video clip of Lisa giving him head, but quickly clicked away because she didn't want to see his dick.

Another video caught her eye since she recognized the sofa. She pressed play and saw her friend going down on her brother. Unique never mentioned sucking dick before, but there she was. Reign grimaced when her brother obviously came in her mouth. She laughed as she took off to wash her mouth. Reef propped the phone up while she was away and spoke into it.

"Shorty got some good ass pussy" he vowed enthusiastically.

"Wow" was all Reign could say when she watched her brother dip between Unique's thighs and eat her out. She was in pain, but that didn't stop her from getting soaking wet from the display. A wave a jealously washed over her when her friend busted a whimpering nut in her brother's mouth. Reef wasted no time and rushed inside of her. She felt another tinge of jealously watching Reef make slow, sweet love to Unique.

They lovingly tongue kissed as he stroked her. Unique came once more just before he did.

"No wonder you got her pregnant!" she told him as he obviously came inside of her. Her face twisted at the memory of sex with Kidd. He would roughly enter and hump until he came. No after tongue kisses like Reef and Reign were doing.

"Yo, you my girl from now on," he declared while still inside of her.

"What about Lisa?" she asked and held her breath.

"Fuck her. You with me now." Reign had nothing more to see or say. She laid the phone on her chest and went to sleep.

—————

"**M**y girl Reign, bring the pain in the rain, say my name," Sharon rapped when

she came back in the hospital room hours later.

"Ma? What's wrong with you?" Reign asked and sat up in her bed. She had heard her mother rapping along to some of the old school rap songs from her day when they came on the radio, but never bust a freestyle.

"Ain't nothing wrong with me!" she shouted, slurred and wobbled. Her breath crossed the room before she did and hit Reign in her nose.

"You been drinking?" she asked despite it now being obvious. "You drunk!"

"Yeah she is. Come on, mama. We gotta get you outa here before anyone see you like this," her friend said. She saw her stagger in and rushed to check on her.

"Where we going, chica? Oooh, let's get a drink!" Sharon said and tried to dance with her.

"No more drinks, mama," she said and steered her towards the door.

Her coworker turned to Reign and said, "She's good. Get some rest."

"OK," she said and watched her take her mother away. She saw something fall from her open purse, but waited until they were gone before climbing down to retrieve it.

"Oww, oww, oww!' she whined and winced when she felt all her aches and pains. She picked it up and tried to make sense of the pregnancy test.

"Yoooo, my moms is pregnant?"

Reign ignored most of the incoming calls until she saw the name 'Neek' appear on the screen with what must have been her vagina. It wouldn't make sense for her brother to assign any one else's pussy to her name. She couldn't help but to answer it. Mainly because she missed her friend.

"Sup," she barked into the line. Unique paused in confusion when the call was answered then hung up. Reign hit the call log and called right back.

"Hello?" Unique pleaded, hoping it was Reef. She'd had some really vivid bad dreams before and awoke to a better day. She hoped and prayed this was just one of them. She was gonna be the best baby mama ever.

"You just called my brother phone!" she said harsher than intended.

"Cuz, I wanted to hear his voice on the voicemail," she explained without explaining she'd been doing it all day. It was all that was left of her first love.

"Oh OK. I heard about what you did. On 170th, " she said, meaning "thanks".

"Yeah, I had to represent. When they letting you go?" she asked.

"Not for a minute. Gotta make sure I ain't got no internal injuries and shit. You coming down here?" she asked hopefully.

"You want me to come down there?" Unique asked just as hopeful.

"I asked your big head, didn't I!" she shot back making it official. "And bring some weed!"

"OK" she cheered and got sad once more. Reef had just left her with a big bag of fluffy buds the day he died. She and Simone had smoked half of it already. As long as Simone was high she wasn't fussing about the baby. "I'm on my way!"

The block was subdued as the residents mourned one of their own. Reef was the man around here and things wouldn't be the same until the next man stepped up and took over.

Smart money said it would be Tito. Being Reef's right hand man, he was expected to keep the block moving. Most of all, he was expected to avenge the blood loss. Violence begets violence and it was expected. The whole hood was watching, he had to do something.

"Sup, yo. Let's go back over to 170th Street!" Neta said,

speaking for the entire group of girls behind her. "We ready to smash these bitches!"

"Word," Unique replied. She was down to walk back up Ogden and fight them again.

"I'll shoot a head up with anyone of them bum broads!" Jewel declared. She pounded her fist into her palm as she spoke and hyped Unique even more.

"Chill, yo. We gotta wait 'til Reign come home. They did her dirty, yo," she relented.

"Why they jumped her? What she was doing up there anyway? Where you was?" all the girls clamored at once. Unique couldn't answer most of their questions and repeated they had to wait 'til Reign got out the hospital. They had to wait 'til she got home, but she planned to get answers today.

————

"Sup," Unique greeted when Reign woke up from her second nap of the day.

"Sup. How long you been here?" she asked, seeing night had fell outside her window.

"'Bout five minutes," she lied since she had been there for a couple of hours. "We can't smoke in here!"

"I know," Reign admitted. She looked around and saw her mother still hadn't returned. "Yo, guess who pregnant, too?"

"You!" she said excitedly then frowned. "By Kidd?"

"Hell no!" she spat. "That bitch ass nigga had them girls jump me. He tricked me to coming on the block, talking 'bout Reef killed his brother."

"You think he had something to do with it?" Unique quickly surmised. She watched as her friend processed it and nodded her head.

"You know what? He probably did! Ain't nobody seen Tito? He left with my brother."

"I just seen them when I left. He was with Black and them,"

she said. She could tell by the looks on their faces they had murder on their minds.

"Well, if they don't get him, I will," she growled. "And them dirty chicks that jumped me!"

"Word! The whole crew was down to go up there just now!" she recalled.

"Who was it?" Reign asked eagerly. It's always good to know who really has your back so you can have theirs. No sense riding for people who don't deserve it.

"Girl, it was Neta, Cardi, Jewel," she said, naming names causing her smile to grow with each one.

"Yo, y'all gotta wait for me!" Reign pleaded.

"That's what I said! Yo, we ain't even gone look they way until you come home. Make them think we scared," she said as the lesson came to mind.

"Rock they ass to sleep!" they both cheered like Reef had taught them. He schooled them in the art of ghetto warfare before they were old enough to understand what it was. It was one of many lessons that would explain itself when the opportunity and occasions arouse.

"Man, that's fucked up they killed him!" Unique snapped from anger and sorrow. "I loved him, yo! I did! You think I was creeping, but I loved him!"

"He loved you, too. I know he did," Reign said. The video was proof enough that he planned to leave Lisa for her. "Sorry I hit you."

"We good. I love you, mama," Unique and rushed over to hug her neck.

"Love you too, chica," she said as she hugged. It was all good until she hugged a little too hard. "Oww, oww, oww."

"My bad!" she reeled and pulled away. "Yo, this thing on wheels. Let's go outside!"

"Come on!" Reign agreed and gingerly got out the bed. She grimaced and winced and pulled her I.V bag behind her as they snuck out the hall. They made it to the stairs and down to the parking lot.

Unique sparked up a blunt and passed it to her friend. They alternated the standard two tokes and passed it back and forth until the weed was gone. They talked about any and everything like always, but Reign had one question nagging at her. Just before they went back in she stopped and asked.

"What does it feel like? When you came. What does it feel like?" she asked intently.

"Like electric butterflies fluttering around in my soul!" she said and closed her eyes as if she could feel it now. "But wait, didn't you tell me Kidd had you cumming like crazy?"

"I lied! That shit was so whack," she said now that she had something to compare it to.

She felt creepy watching the video a second time, but that didn't stop her from watching it again. The session set the bar for what she wanted next time she gave it up. It wouldn't be Kidd either because Kidd was about to be dead.

Chapter 12

The men of 164th Street all listened intently as Tito explained how he and Reef set out and only he came back. His delay of a whole day had him looking suspect, so he spoke clear and slow as if his life depended on it. Mainly because it did.

"I'm one hunnid percent sure it was that nigga Woody. I know that whack ass car with them big ugly ass rims anywhere," he repeated.

"But that don't even make no sense? Woody?" Jack, one of their crew asked.

"He was driving, but some young light skin dude was bussing," he replied.

"So why you ain't bust back? And why would they bust anyway?" Jack asked and leaned in for an answer.

"Yo, that shit was personal. Reef killed his brother. This was get back for big C," he explained since he no longer had to keep the secret.

"Well, march your ass over there and kill both of them niggas! Hurry up before Reef get lonely!" Jack demanded and they were as good as dead.

Now that he explained to the men, he had to go break it to his woman. Lisa opened on the first knock and he wrapped her into his arms.

"Nothing I could do, mama," he said to her, but kept holding her too tight and too long.

She grimaced and pushed away when she felt his dick get hard. Tito was so freaked out he was fucked up. He fucked all the young girls by supplying them with more weed and alcohol than their young systems could handle. Then he would slide up in their young pussies without permission. He'd fuck Lisa too if she would let him. The closest he got was jacking off while sniffing her panties when they were teens.

"What I'ma do now?" she moaned, but meant who would take care of her now. She was a kept woman and needed someone to keep her. She would keep their dick sucked as her part of the bargain.

"I know we need his coke connect. Mines charges twice as much," he sighed. He planned to take Reef's spot and needed the connect.

"Who, Tariq? Oooh, Tariq!" she cheered since he was fine and rich. He could definitely get next. "I don't know his number tho? It's in his phone."

"I gotta get that phone!"

———

Woody and Kidd went about their lives unaware of the plans in motion to end them. Woody would most likely go first since he was always riding around in his loud ass car blasting loud ass music. Kidd usually hugged the trap like a hippy hugs trees. He didn't go far since the trap was booming and Leticia fucked at the drop of a dime. She was nowhere near as pretty, fine, or clean as Reign, but she was always down to fuck and suck and that counts for something.

"Yo, little cousin. You feel like riding across the bridge with us? Some new chick hit me up. She said bring a friend."

"I'm getting this money, yo," Kidd said. Any and every child of a crackhead who has went to bed hungry would always put money over anything.

"More for me," he shrugged and hopped in his Jetta. Kidd went back to slinging crack while Woody set off in search of new pussy. He turned on Ogden and passed right by Lisa who actually made the call. She made another call to Tito up the block.

"Here he come. Give him one for me," she growled.

"I'ma give him one for errbody on the block," he said and pulled a Mac-10 from his backpack. The thundering car system announced he was coming before he got there.

"I bomb atomically! Socrates philosophies and hypotheses," Woody rapped along with the Wu-Tang Clan coming out of his system.

It looked like life hit the mute button when Tito stepped out and began firing. He could see the flash and feel the pain, but the 'brrr' of the machine gun didn't reach him. The slugs did and slumped him over his steering wheel. The car blew the red light and got T-boned by a taxi. The wreck gave Tito a diversion to make a clean getaway. He rounded the corner and hopped in his car to make his escape. That was one down and one to go.

————

"Pull out!" Simone moaned when Bryan's stroke slowed to a slow drag, meaning he was about to come. She now knew his body well enough to tell him when he was cumming before he knew himself. Usually she would clamp her walls down, grip that dick and milk it dry.

"Oh yeah? Ugh!" he grunted and snatched himself out of her gushy pussy without a second to spare. He used her juice to stroke himself and bust on her belly. The both leaned and looked at the explosive cum shot. Globs of pearly white cum coated her flat, brown stomach.

"Whew, that was close!"

"Mmhm," she hummed at the futile display. She was already pregnant on purpose, but now she could say it was his fault. This was her third pregnancy since giving birth to Unique, but unlike the others, this one was planned. This one she was keeping. Her daughter being pregnant at the same time wasn't going to interfere with her plans. She caught her a good guy with some bread and promptly trapped him with a baby. Unique wasn't going to mess this up for her.

"Might be too late anyway cuz I'm late."

"Late for what?" he asked, ready to give her a ride. He had to get home to his wife and kids anyway.

"Late for my period!" she huffed as if irritated. "Last thing I need is another baby. Especially when my daughter pregnant, too!"

"Unique is fucking? I mean, pregnant?" he reeled. He liked checking her out whenever he saw her, but didn't think she was sexually active.

"Man, yes. By her friend's brother who just got murdered," she said and rattled on. Bryan missed most of it while conspiring on hitting Unique himself. It shouldn't be hard if she was a gold digger like her mom.

"Well, I'll take care of it if you are pregnant," he said just like she hoped even if it wasn't what he meant. She was thinking him moving in and taking care of them while he was thinking abortion.

"Thank you, baby. I know you will," she sighed happily and happily kissed her way downtown. The miscommunication got his dick sucked once more for the road.

———

"**Y**o, mad people owe my brother money!" Reign said when Unique came in and sat down. She had checked the ledger on the phone and calculated what he owed and was owed. Tito owed him five grand, but he owed twice that to Rankin. The few hundreds scattered amongst the dope boys on the block balanced the ledger out perfectly.

"Word," Unique said and sighed from a distance greater than just being across the room. Today was the day they had to bury her first love and baby daddy to the baby he would never see.

"I know, right?" Reign said and twisted her lips when she filled in the blank look on her friend's face. It was bad enough to have to go put her brother in the ground, but she still had to deal with her drunken mother. Sharon came to her room daily whether on duty or not, but smelled like liquor either way.

"Hey, girls," Sharon greeted as she entered the hospital room. Both girls squinted to see if she had been drinking. Both were relieved that she hadn't been.

"Hey, ma. Good morning, Miss Brown," they greeted together before Reign took the lead. "You signed me out? I'm ready to go!"

"Yes and I bet you are," she said and came to inspect her child's face. She was under inspection too as Reign sniffed for alcohol. A long week later and she was finally headed home. Her color was coming back but she still had some more healing to do.

"You healing up nicely."

"You too," she shot back since her mother wasn't drunk. Sharon paused at the quip, then kept it moving. She deserved it for going out bad, but she was back.

"Yeah, well no sense in getting better to go back fighting again," Sharon warned since she knew her child was with child. She knew her child could be wild too and had no doubt she wanted some get back.

"Yeah, OK," she huffed. Reign and Unique twisted their lips at the fallacy. Reign changed into the clothes her mother brought up to the hospital and they stepped outside.

"I'm going to get Reef's car from that girl today. No sense in us walking while she can't even drive," Sharon said.

"Word!" Reign cosigned as if they walked over to the train for the long ride up to Woodlawn Cemetery. Unique kept her mouth shut since she'd seen Tito driving it this morning. Her hand went to her stomach where his child was forming as a silent protest.

"I need to tell you something, Miss Brown," Unique blurted when the courage came to a head on the train. She couldn't hold it any longer and the truth spilled out of her mouth.

"I'm pregnant," she said and let her digest that before feeding her the rest.

"You ain't the only one," Reign quipped quite snippily. Her mother shot her glance, but she rolled her eyes.

"No, you're not the only. Anyway, have you told the child's father? Is he going to be able to help?" Sharon shot back and squinted at her daughter to see what she had going on.

"I told him, but—" she said, but it was all she was able to get out before breaking down.

"She and Reef was messing around. It's his baby," Reign tossed in from the side. Her mean teen attitude against her mother was back and she got a kick out of the shocked look on her face.

"You? I mean how?" she stammered and struggled to find the words. Unique knew what she was asking and answered.

"I'm 100% sure. I ain't been with no one else," she said almost truthfully. She'd been with others before Reef came along, but he was the only one who came inside of her.

"On my sofa!" Sharon frowned when she remembered a crusty sex stain a few weeks back. Unique said yes by blinking and ducking her head. A slow smile spread on her face at the notion of another grandchild. She barely saw the one she had because she couldn't stand it's mother. Meanwhile, she was like a mother to Unique and would be there for this one.

"Wouldn't it be crazy if y'all have y'all kids on the same day!" Reign cut in to spoil the moment.

"Both who?" both Sharon and Unique asked with matching frowns. Reign decided to answer her friend since her mother was close enough to hear.

"My moms, yo. She pregnant too!" she said. Unique almost got whiplash from snapping her head towards Sharon.

"Miss Sharon!" she shrieked. Sharon was just as dumbfounded.

"Me! Where you get that from?" she asked with another frown.

"You dropped your pregnancy test at the hospital, yo. When you was drunk!" Reign shot back. Sharon now knew what happened to it. She had no idea where it was but she couldn't find it.

"Nah, chica. I tested your pee when you were laid up in that bed. I'm not pregnant, you are!" she shot back. Reign crossed her arms and balled up her face for the rest of the ride.

———

The family didn't do church, so the service was held at the gravesite. If there was any consolation to burying a child it's seeing how many people loved him in life. Reef was a street rock star and all five boroughs were represented. Dudes and broads all dolled up in latest fashions and gaudy jewelry.

"There's Uncle Raw," Reign said, pointing at her uncle standing front and center. Those were the first words she'd spoken since getting fussed at on the train. She couldn't wait to get home and take another pregnancy test so she could shut her mother up.

Uncle Raw was the only remnant of her father's side of the family. He lived in Brooklyn, but made sure to pop in from time to time. Sharon couldn't help but notice how much the man looked like her ex husband. Especially now that he was seething mad.

"Hey, Sharon. I'm so sorry," Raw said and hugged her tightly. He let her go and scooped Reign and Unique in a group hug. He always saw them together when he came to visit so he hugged them together.

"Who did it?"

"I'on know," Reign replied, causing her mother to snap her head in her direction. She knew her daughter well enough to know when she was lying. And that shoulder hunch and girly voice was a dead giveaway.

She held her tongue because she was waiting and hoping for the street to avenge her child's blood. Tito got one a couple days ago and was laying on the other one to show his face.

Kidd was spooked since Woody got swiss-cheesed up the block. He and Leticia stayed indoors to smoke weed and fuck while his mother slung rocks for him. He may have been stupid, but smart enough not to go outside.

"Let me know if you find out if you hear. You hear me?" he told Reign since she would know before her mother would.

"OK, Unc. Have you umm, talk to my father?" she asked trailing off to a whisper. Uncle Raw turned to pay attention to the service, but passed her a letter. Reign could feel her father's presence through the envelope. Her heart skipped a beat just seeing his handwriting. The tears that ran down her cheek were as much from the memory of riding on her daddy's shoulders than her dead brother in the box.

Reef's old basketball coach gave the eulogy despite him going in the opposite direction. Both Reign and Unique missed most of it from their own thoughts and memories of the man in the casket.

Lisa and Tito walked briskly towards the gravesite just before Reef was lowered into his final resting spot. She would have been there on time since she had his car but it needed to be washed.

"Fuck this bitch got on, yo?" Reign growled at the mid-thigh mini dress she had on. It dipped low in the front to show off the plump Puerto Rican titties. She was in mourning, but dressed for the night. She knew there would be some ballers in the place. It wasn't cheating if she fucked one of them since Reef was dead and almost buried.

"Fucking slut," Unique snarled and touched her stomach. It was months from being round but she knew what was in there.

Even Sharon cocked her head curiously as Lisa made her rounds receiving condolences and phone numbers before even paying respects to the guest of honor. The three watched in disgust as the girl flirted with the ballers. It was bad enough already, but got worse when Reign looked up and locked eyes with trouble.

"What?" Unique asked when she saw the look on her face. She followed her eyes and saw Rankin.

Chapter 13

Everyone came to show respect to the young hood hero, but no one paid much attention as he was lowered into the ground. Life is for the living, so they focused on what to do after the service. 164th planned to hold a block party in his honor, so most would smoke and drink to the man's memory.

Quite a few ballers schemed on smashing Lisa since she was slinging her big Puerto Rican ass all over the funeral. A few more plotted on Reef's vacant spot in the drug trade. Rankin's red eyes scanned the crowd with one agenda. He wanted his money. Dead isn't the same as bankruptcy and he still expected to get paid.

"Sup, Dred. We just getting here," Tito said and extended a hand. Rankin scoffed at it, but still gave him a pound. He made it a few pounds heavier when he gripped his hand and spoke.

"Mi need mi money today," he practically growled. He glared over at Reign then back into Tito's soul.

"Huh? Oh, yeah. Um, I had paid Reef, but you see—" he lied and looked towards the grave. He buckled under the man's stare and decided against trying to stiff him.

"Yeah, fall though. We got you. We need to keep the dough flowing."

"Hmp," Rankin huffed. He would love to keep that outlet, but wasn't sure about Tito and the rest. Reef had been gone a week and he hadn't heard nothing about his ten grand.

Everyone knew Reef had a ton of cash stashed somewhere and the hunt was on. Lisa turned her apartment upside down, but only came up with a few miscellaneous bands. On the contrary, Sharon couldn't bring herself to enter her sons bedroom. Reign couldn't wait to get home and explore.

"Hey, Tariq," Lisa sang when she came up on Reef's coke connect. It was a little too flirty for his woman who frowned to show it.

"Sorry about your loss," he said, trying to ignore her cleavage. Her nipples got stiff in his presence because money always turned her on.

"Me too. Make sure you come over to the block. We're having something in his honor," she said in parting. She put on a dazzling display as she walked away.

"Tramp," Tariq's girl snapped at the inappropriate way she came on to him.

"Yeah," he agreed. He too hoped one of Reef's people would be able to keep business going.

The funeral ended when Reef reached the bottom of the hole. People turned and made their way out of the cemetery. Sharon had to rush to catch up with Lisa as she practically sprinted to the parking lot.

"Lisa! Hey Lisa!" she called and caught up just as she reached Reef's car. "I wanted to see my grandson and we need a ride."

"Um, I ain't going straight back to the block," she dismissed and hopped in the passenger seat. Poor Tito looked confused as to what he was supposed to do. Until his cousin screamed at him that is. "Get in the car nigga!"

"Yo, that bitch is mad foul!" Reign snarled. She dreaded the long train ride back to High Bridge as much as she hated watching her brother's car leaving without them. Sharon was too shocked for words and too proud for tears, so she shrugged and turned towards the train.

"Y'all need a ride, Mrs. Brown?" Black asked when he saw them. It was a rhetorical question that he answered himself by hopping out and opening the doors for them.

"Thank you, sweetheart," she said as she sat in the passenger seat. Reign thanked him when she slid in beside him, but Unique stayed mute. He pulled off and headed south.

"Thank you again, sweetheart," Sharon said when they reached the block.

"No problem. Reef was my man. If y'all need anything, just let me know!" he insisted.

"Look-it," Unique said and nodded up just the street. There was Reef's car parked right in front of Lisa's building. They had come straight from the cemetery, so that meant she did too for them to beat them back.

"Yo, I ain't going out like that," Reign growled. She had no idea what she could do, but she was going to do something.

"We should beat that bitch ass," Unique suggested but got shot down.

"Leave her alone. She'll get hers," Sharon said. She led the way into the building and up to the apartment. As usual, she retired to her room to rest for work. Reign and Unique went outside to smoke a blunt.

"What you gone do if you are pregnant? By Kidd?" Unique blurted. Even she knew his days were numbered and coming to an end.

"First of all, I'm not pregnant, so ain't nothing to talk about," she spat so forcefully, so Unique let it go. Especially since Neta and the rest of the crew spotted them and made a beeline over.

"Sup, let's go step to them bum bitches right now!" Neta said as she gave Reign a pound. She was already hot about her girl getting jumped, but seeing the remnants of the ass kicking on her face made it worse.

"I'm down, but not today. Doctor said I gotta go easy for a minute," she replied.

"Word, word," Jewel nodded and passed a blunt. "But if any one them hoes step foot on the block tonight—"

She didn't finish the statement but didn't have to. If Leticia or any girl tried to come to the memorial block party they would be having one of their own. Reign locked eyes on Tito as he approached, so she knew he was coming to talk to her.

"Yo, let me holla at you for a second," he said, stopping at a distance away from her nosey friends. She wanted to talk to him anyway and quickly came over.

"Yo, you owed my brother five bands. My moms need that," she insisted although Sharon would never see it.

"Nah, I paid him that already. He must not have marked me off," he said since he knew his friend kept records. "I need to get the rest of the bread so I can pay Rankin."

"Rest of what bread?" she asked genuinely.

"The dough he had in the crib. We need it to keep business popping. And his phone," he replied when he noticed it in her hand.

"Yo, I'on know nothing about no money and this my phone," she shot back. Tito shot a glanced up the block and saw it was too many people outside for him to snatch it away from her.

"A'ight, yo," he relented momentarily. He still planned to get that phone and the fortune he knew his partner left behind. He watched Reign's booty movement as she walked away and decided he wanted some of that, too. The block was about to be his and everything on it.

"What that nigga want?" Yvette asked first since she had sex with him. Last night in fact, for some of the weed they were smoking now.

"Same thing he always want!" Neta huffed. She was a little salty that he never pushed up on her again after sexing her on the roof over the summer.

"And what he'll never get," Reign vowed. At that moment, she swore no one would ever get it again since the one guy she gave it up to killed her brother. A sigh escaped at the thought of actually being pregnant by Kidd. She planned to boost another test first chance she got. It would have to wait since the DJ was beginning to set up. 164th Street was about to have a block party.

———

"I don't guess it would do any good to tell you to keep your ass in the house would it?" Sharon quipped as she she packed her yogurt and juice for work. She could hear the clamour of the party beginning to grow on the street below.

"Probably not," Reign shot back sarcastically then switched up. "It's for my brother."

"Yeah, well at least I don't have to worry about you getting pregnant any more," Sharon shot back. She was ready to go wherever the girl wanted to take it. They locked eyes to see if tonight was the night. Reign rolled her eyes and walked away putting the inevitable on pause, for now.

Sharon held her head high and stepped outside. She marched up the block towards the bus deflecting comments from her son's friends. Reign watched and waited for her bus like always except for a different reason. As soon as the bus passed, she headed to her brother's room. She took a deep breath and walked inside.

"Dang, you was fly!" she cheered as she looked into his packed closet. He had all the latest clothes, sneakers and boots in pristine condition. It was well known the Reef had that bag and the search was on to find it.

Street people keep cash in shoe boxes, so she went through the fifty stacked in his closet. She came up with just under a thousand dollars and his personal weed stash. She almost got a buzz just sniffing the fruity colored buds through the bag. Two boxes contained guns and the ammo that went in them. He had taught her how to use both. She screwed the long silencer on one and pointed the laser sight around the room.

"Pow," she said and pretended to shoot his baby mama between her colored contacts. A knock on the door put her treasure hunt on hold, for now.

"Guess who pregnant?" Unique shouted when Reign opened the door for her. She rushed in and repeated, " Guess who pregnant, yo?"

"Bitch, errbody we know fucking!" she laughed instead of trying to guess. Having a baby was a matter of when, not who since eventually they would all have little human anchors holding them back.

"My moms, yo! That dude Bryan done knocked her ass up! And she was fussing at me!" Unique laughed. She had just revealed it to her before she left and she couldn't wait to go tell her friend.

"Well, as long as I ain't, I don't care who else got knocked up," she shot back. A little calculation determined she was late for her last period. She wrote it off as part of getting her ass whipped.

"Yeah, OK," Unique said with a squint since she saw through her act. Reign was worried and it showed.

"Roll up!" she said to change the subject from her womb. She took notice of Unique's skin tight jeans and shirt Unique wore, knowing she wouldn't be able to fit them much longer when her belly grew. She rushed off to get fly herself despite the bruises still visible on her face.

"OK, look at you!" Unique cheered when Reign came back

fly. Her own skin tight jeans displayed the spread of her hips and fat crotch. The tight T-shirt showed off plump breast but what stood out most was her brother's diamond name plate.

"Gonna represent!" she said proudly. They smoked a blunt together before stepping outside so they wouldn't have to share.

———

"Yo, Tariq just pulled up," Lisa announced from her front stoop where she and Tito sat. The party was in full swing and guests were coming in droves.

"Damn, there go Rankin, too. I gotta holla at bruh. Don't let Tariq leave before I can talk to him," Tito said and rushed off.

"I got him, yo," she assured him and stood. She was right too because Tariq made a beeline to her as soon as he saw her. Meanwhile, Tito rushed over and hopped in Rankin's car to handle business.

"Sup, rude mon!" Tito said in a mock Jamaican accent that pissed the dred off.

"You from yard?" he challenged. "Mi not chat Spanish to you, do I?"

"My bad, yo. Here," he said and switched the subject by passing him a bag of cash.

Rankin frowned at the large bag of small bills. Reef always laundered bills enough to pay in hundreds instead of the wads of ones and flocks of fives, tens and twenties. He didn't know he had to press the dealers on the block to pay up. Most had the same idea he had about keeping what was owed to Reef. Tito was able to convince them to pay up so they could re-up.

They got down to the business of keeping the flow of weed flowing through the block. If they had to go through Perez or any other middleman, they would have to pay the middleman tax. Meanwhile, Lisa stalled Tariq so Tito could try to work a deal with him, too.

"Come," Lisa said, reaching for Tariq's hand. He cast a

glance around to see who could see him. The group of young girls watching them didn't register, so he took her hand and let her lead him away.

"You see that shit?" Jewel asked first. "Yo, she mad foul!"

"Who?" Reign asked as she and Unique made their appearance. The diamond name plate stole the show and changed the subject.

"Yo! That shit is dope!" Neta sang like she never saw it before. She had but never this close since she could never get next to Reef. They were chatting about the chain when Lisa got Tariq up to the roof.

"What you got me up here for?" Tariq laughed knowingly, but still scanned for danger. He had a gun tucked right next to his dick and wasn't sure which one he needed to pull out. He was down to bust either one.

"For this," she said as she lowered before him like an altar. She worshipped the all mighty dollar and sucking dick got her closer to her lord.

"Word," he smiled as she pulled him from his pants. His dick was semi soft when she reached it but rock hard by the time it reached her mouth.

"Hmmm," she hummed, knowingly when she recognized the taste of pussy left behind from a last second quickie before he left home. Tariq's girl often fucked him right before he left to keep him from fucking other chicks. It worked most of the time but was powerless against blowjobs.

"OK then," he chuckled at her dazzling dick sucking display. She planted loud kisses all over the head while tugging on his shaft. He got into it and began rocking in and out of her mouth to the beat playing below.

Lisa moved her hands to his hips to brace herself while he fucked her face. She could only hope Tito handled his business because Tariq was certainly handling his. His increased moans and choppy stroke was a prelude to him busting a nut on her tonsils.

"Shit girl!" he exclaimed as they locked eyes while she swallowed. He pushed his dick around in her mouth until he was empty and pulled it away.

"You like that?" she purred as she rose and faced him. "Been wanting to do that since I first seen you."

"Hells yeah! I wasn't expecting that. I really came to see who gonna handle business since your man gone," he said unaware that's what the free blowjob was about.

"My cousin Tito. He was Reef's right hand man," she replied and led the way back out. She hoped he was done so they could talk business. Reign and her girls were in front of her building when they arrived. Tito flirted with them all not knowing they were coming to confront Lisa.

"Sup, yo," Tito greeted when Lisa came out and made the introduction. The two men shook and stepped off to handle business. "Let's take a walk."

"Bet," Tariq said and followed him away from the DJ set up so they wouldn't have to yell.

"Fuck y'all down here for?" Lisa said to shoo the girls off. She noticed Reign wearing the chain and demanded it. "I'ma need that chain, yo. I bought that for him,"

"No, you didn't!" Reign shot back since she was there when he ordered it. "And you need to come off them keys. That's my brother's car!"

"That whip in my name. Now run along and I'll come for my chain later," she said and stepped forward. The girls took a step back because none of them wanted to tangle with her. Not yet anyway.

"Dang, her breath stink!" Unique frowned when she smelled the hot cum mixed with menthol on her breath. They all went back closer to the DJ to dance and flirt since it was a party after all.

Chapter 14

Reef's going away party was jumping, but that didn't prevent a couple of people from sneaking off. A couple of couples snuck off to fuck while others had other plans. Black and Goose stepped to the end of the block and came around on 163rd.

"Taxi!" Black called as a gypsy cab ambled up the block. The weary driver didn't like picking up young black men since they had a tendency of putting guns to their heads and taking their money. Black overcame the man's fears by waving cold cash in hand. He was alone so the driver took a shot and pulled over.

"Where to?" he asked as his passenger slid into the backseat. He realized his error when Goose came out of the shadows and hopped in, too. And just like the driver feared Black pulled a gun and pressed it to the back of his head.

"170th," Black said as the driver pulled off while Goose pulled a Tech-9 a nd cocked it.

"I have kids," the driver pleaded as he drove. He scanned the streets for a patrol car hoping for intervention. He planned to run a light or ram head first into it to get attention.

"Chill, papi. No one gone hurt you," Black assured even though it was clear they planned to do something to somebody.

"Just take the money. You can have the car. Just let me—"

"Bruh, shut the fuck up. Please!" Goose laughed then turned deadly serious when he spotted his target.

"Yo, Leticia hurry up," Kidd demanded just as she stepped from the store. He relaxed enough to hit his own block to trap. He had no choice since his mother kept running off with his dope.

"Boy don't ru—" she began, but saw the barrel pointed in her direction. Kidd turned to see what turned her face from yellow to white just as Goose tugged on the trigger.

The driver kept driving as he leaned out the open window and let them have it. Kidd pulled Leticia in front of him as a shield and pulled his own gun. Four rounds dropped her to the concrete leaving him exposed. She stared up at the afterlife when her soul leaked out the bullet holes. He fired back, but got hit in his neck and fell under a barrage of gunfire. Kidd gripped the hole in his neck, trying to keep his life liquid inside his body.

"Back to 163rd," Black ordered to the shook up driver. He'd seen and done a lot in these Bronx streets, but this was his first time committing a drive by. He circled the block and headed back where he came from.

"What you seen, papi?" Goose asked as they reached their destination.

"Me no see nada!" he declared.

"My man," Black congratulated and passed him a hundred dollar bill. He accepted it with shaky hands and let his passengers out. They walked over a block to their own block where the block party was still going on. News of the drive by slowly circulated on the block. Reef's murder was avenged, but Reign and Unique couldn't rejoice. Reef wasn't coming back no matter who got killed.

"Yo, I'm going upstairs," Reign announced and turned to leave. Unique was mourning too, so she couldn't provide much comfort. She headed the other way and entered her own building.

Reign had her head down as she walked inside her building. She heard footsteps behind her and assumed it was Unique.

"We may as well smoke another one, huh?" she said behind her without looking back.

"Ya mon," came a deep voice causing Reign to spin and see a red-eyed Rankin standing behind her. He closed the distance between them in a flash and wrapped her into his arms.

"Chill, B!'" she whined and squirmed to try and free herself. He was either too strong or she was too weak because she couldn't get away.

"You ask Rankin for hundred dollar for a fuck. Mi lose five hundred, but not get no sweet poom-poom," he slurred and licked her face.

"Chill! I got my period!" she pleaded. She realized just how helpless she was at that moment.

"Mi not scared of no blood," he said and shoved his thick tongue in her mouth. There was no bell to save her, but luckily Tito came in when he did. He too was hoping to catch her alone, but her vagina was last on his list. He wanted Reef's stash of cash and phone full of contacts.

"Stop," Reign pleaded once again and once again struggled to get free.

"Sup, yo?" Tito called out, putting pause on a rape. Rankin pulled away quickly and reached without pulling his strap.

"Nothing 'appening 'ere," he declared, raising his hands. Reign took advantage of the reprieve and ran upstairs and inside her apartment. The sound of multiple locks echoed in the hallway.

Reign was so shaken up, she grabbed one her new guns and dove under her covers to hide. Sleep crept up on her just as quickly as morning.

———

"Reign, get up. Come on, here," Sharon insisted as she barged into her daughter's room. She pulled the shade to flood the room with sunlight. There was a dare in her tone hoping for a problem.

"Chill, ma! What you doing? Dang!" she fussed. She really fussed when her mother snatched the comforter away. She scrambled to cover the gun before she saw it. "What ma!"

"Don't what me. Get yo' ass up and pee on this!" she demanded, thrusting a fresh pregnancy test in her face.

"You bugging, yo," she shot, but did have to pee. She rolled out of bed to kill two birds with one stone. She would relieve her bladder and shut up all the pregnancy talk at the same time. She snatched the test strip from her hand and started for the door.

"Un uh. You don't snatch shit from me little girl. Now put it back and try again," she said, extending her open palm. They locked eyes for a second before Reign did what she was told. That's all it took for her to realize her mother wasn't playing with. She tried again and plucked it from her hand and stomped off.

"Keep trying me, yo. I'll beat that bitch ass," she mumbled really low as she peed loudly on the strip. Pee got on her fingers but she didn't care. She wiped, stood and came out to find her mother in the hallway.

"Gimme," she said. Obviously she didn't care about a little pee either and took it in her bare hand.

"And why my kitchen ain't clean?" Sharon spat next so she would have something to do during the fifteen minute wait.

Five minutes later, it was clear she intended to bitch and moan the whole way. Reign balled her face up and stomped into the kitchen to clean up the dishes she left overnight. She back talked, but only in her mind and waited on the results so she could shut her up. The egg timer dinged and time was up. Sharon looked at the test then her daughter. She handed Reign the test strip and asked, "Please tell me you know who the father is?"

"I, I—,"she stammered, but couldn't get the words out. This was one of the few times in history that knowing who the father was was actually worse than not knowing.

"I only been with one person," she said with eye contact.

It didn't make it much better, so Sharon went back to her room to drink. Reign too had something to make her feel better so she grabbed her phone and called her. Unique didn't answer the first call, so she picked up her father's letter to read it. She traced her dad's handwriting on the return address of Clinton correctional facility. Tears clouded her vision once more so she put the letter in her panty drawer and tried her phone again. Again she got no answer so she tried again.

"Girl, what!" Unique fussed when she awoke from the fifth call. Now that she was awake she could hear Bryan and her mother fucking in the next room. He was getting his 'one for the road' before going home to his family.

"Man you not gone believe this shit!" Reign proclaimed since she could hardly believe it herself.

"Just tell me please so I can go back to sleep! I hope Bryan hurry up and bust a nut too!" Unique groaned.

"Yo, I don't even wanna know what that means!" she laughed then got on with it.

"Guess who pregnant by the nigga who killed her brother?"

"Who? No! Say word?" Unique demanded and popped up in her bed. "Yo, I'm on my way over there!" Unique rolled off the bed and went to relieve her bladder. She heard the sounds of sex as she passed her mother's room.

"Whose pussy is this?" he wanted to know. She twisted her lips when she heard her mother answer.

"It's your pussy! Get it! Get, it!" Simone proclaimed.

Unique just should her head. If she had a dollar for every dude she heard her mother say that to she could at least buy a bag of weed on her way over. She cleaned up and announced her departure as she left the front door.

"Sup, yo," Seven greeted as Unique walked by. She was still hot about him telling everyone she let him hit, so she lifted her chin and kept walking.

"So, what you gonna do? You keeping it?" Unique asked as soon as Reign let her in. She waited until they reached her room before nodding.

"Yeah, I'm keeping my baby. Kidd dead, so I ain't gotta worry about him. Nobody ever gonna know he the father," she replied and peered at her friend.

"What? I ain't gonna say nothing to nobody! Shoot, we both gonna have a baby by a dead man," Unique said and accepted the blunt. The weight of the statement sucked all the air out of the room so they smoked in silence.

Meanwhile, Sharon quietly got drunk while pondering about her life. She couldn't help but think about the two kids that came in all shot up last night. The dead girl was only 16, which shook her to her core. The child was just a child, but the streets don't give a fuck if you're young or old, male or female. Anybody can and will get it.

The teen boy was barely clinging to life when they brought him in. He had lost so much blood his internal organs were in danger of collapse. Not on her watch though and Sharon took good care of him. If he lived, it would be because of her hard work. Not that life was much better than death for him since police were going to arrest him if he lived. He was literally damned if lived; doomed if he died. She did her part and unknowingly treated the kid who killed her son and impregnated her daughter.

———

"He ain't have no property or nothing on him?" Kidd's mother asked when she arrived at the hospital.

"Huh?" the nurse asked at the odd question.

Most loved one wanted to know how a patient was doing before asking about their property. The woman knew her son was slinging crack when he got shot and wanted any leftovers he may have had. She scored real good when her son Big C got killed. She smoked all the dope she found then spent all his money on more dope once it was gone.

"Well, is he gonna be ok?" she got around to asking.

"He's strong. He has a chance," the nurse said somberly. Kidd's mother lowered her head and slinked away. She turned a quick trick for a ride back to the block. Luckily, cab drivers accepted cash, coins, subway tokens and blow jobs as payment. Once she got home she got high.

"Poor thing," the nurse sighed as the woman hung her head and slinked out of the room.

She assumed she was going home to mope and moan, but she was actually off to get high. Even if he pulled through he was facing prison time for previous charges as well as the new ones. Her son wasn't coming home any time soon, if ever, so she went to search his room for something to smoke or sell to buy something to smoke.

Pretty much the same thing Reign and Unique were doing back at her apartment. They smoked in silence while contemplating their next move. After an internal debate, Reign spoke up and broke the silence.

"Here. It's half. My brother had it in a shoe box," she said and handed her friend four hundred and some odd dollars. It wasn't quite half, but close enough.

"That's it?" Unique said and heard how it sounded. "I mean, where the rest of his bread? He told me he had a quarter mil put up?"

Reef had revealed how much he was sitting on during pillow

talk after one of their trysts. A good nut is like truth serum and will have a man revealing all their secrets. A lesson that would serve the girls well later in life. Reign knew her brother had money but not how much. Neither knew the answer to the quarter million dollar question about where.

"I ain't see no bank papers," Reign said more to herself. "We gonna have to search his room again. Soon as my moms leave for work!"

"Well, we may as well go shopping," Unique suggested. Fall had just fell and winter was close behind. With this extra money they wouldn't have to wear last years coat. Not to mention both would need maternity clothes soon.

"I guess," Reign agreed. Neither was used to having money, so it was begging to be spent. Once Reign got dressed, they stepped out and caught a gypsy cab to the train and the train over to Fordham Road. A few hours later, they headed back home nearly broke.

Chapter 15

Next stop was Reef's room to search some more. Last time they didn't touch the jewelry, but this time each one got a piece. Unique immediately changed out of her cheap nameplate earrings in favor of the one karat diamond studs Reef wore so well. Reign added another chain to her neck.

"What we gone do about Tito?" Unique asked and rubbed her sore elbow from when he pushed her down. She wasn't sure what, but knew he had to pay.

"We can tell Uncle Raw!"

"Nah, he ain't did nothing to Unc. He touched us and we gonna get him," she spat back.

"He gonna be the next nigga head we bust!" Reign declared.

"He getting money too, so he gotta get got. This gonna be a sweet lick!" Unique concluded as they got ready to handle business.

After countless searches of Reef's room, Reign nor Unique found any more cash. Both Reign and Unique had fucked their money up on clothes, food and showing off. Life on 164th began to change each day since it was under new leadership. Tito now allowed crack sales at the end of the block like he suggested to Reef. And just like Reef said, there were now zombies roaming the block day and night. It wouldn't be long until they started turning tricks and breaking in cars.

Speaking of cars, Sharon now had to work doubles since she was single and lost her son's income. She decided it was time to collect his car from Lisa. It sat on the street instead of the garage he used to keep it in. She got tired of the hour long bus journey when it was minutes away by car. She went to see Lisa and made a pleasant appeal, but came home fuming.

"Hey, Lisa. How's my grand baby?" Sharon sang cordially as she approached Lisa sitting on her front stoop smoking a blunt.

"Sup," she greeted and turned her head. It was body language for "beat it" since she didn't care for the woman. She viewed any woman in her man's life as a threat. Reef spent money on his mother and sister, which was less money for her.

"Yeah, OK. So look, I need my son's car. I didn't want it in my name because—" she began, but trailed off because she didn't want to be a hypocrite. She refused to allow him to put the car in her name because it was bought with drug money. It was still bought with drug money but now she needed it.

"Yo, that's my car. It's in my name," she said then turned completely around and gave his mother her back. Body language for "kiss my ass". She got the hint and stormed off.

"That damn girl got me fucked all the way up!" Sharon fussed when she stormed back into the apartment. "Where my Timbs?"

"Who ma?" Reign stood and demanded. She may have been rebellious but couldn't no one else get smart with her mother.

Her mother looking for her boots was a signal she wanted to fight.

"Yeah who?" Unique asked and got up since she stayed down.

"That nasty little Puerto Rican mami. I'm trying to get my son's car and she claiming it's hers since its in her name!" she said and the girls sprang into action.

"What! That bitch ain't paid nary a penny on his whip!" Reign growled. She usually got a side eye for cursing, but Sharon let this one slide. Besides, Lisa was a bitch, so she was right.

"Word!" Unique cosigned like a best friend will. When Reign began to tie her sneakers up extra tight she leaned down and laced hers tightly as well.

Sharon knew they intended to fight the young woman when they removed their hoop earrings and smeared Vaseline on their faces. She went to the window to watch what she knew was coming from above. She thought about the baby in her child's belly, but didn't try to stop her. Reign losing the child wouldn't be the worse thing that could happen. Her getting pregnant in the first place was the worst thing that could happen and it happened.

"There she go!" Unique said loud enough for Lisa to hear. Lisa looked up, saw her pointing at her and stood..

"Yup. Here I am. What's good?" she said throwing her arms wide in an invitation to fight. "You looking for me, I'm right here yo!"

"Yo, you told my moms we can't get my brother whip?" Reign demanded as she approached.

"That's my shit," she shot back and got popped. Reign threw a jab that busted her lip. Unique followed with a sock to the jaw and it was on. They jumped her but she jumped them, as well.

"Come on with it!" Lisa shouted as she traded punches with both girls. Tito wasn't there to break it up and everyone else wanted to watch the show. They got what they came for too as the 'pap, pap, pap' of punches and slaps echoed up the block.

"Oooh shit! They fighting!" Neta shouted and led the charge down the block. She and the rest would have jumped in too, but didn't want problems with Tito.

Reign was lucky to have Unique with her because she couldn't handle the woman on her own. Even with her, it was a pretty even fight as the girls beat each other lumpy and bloody. All three were all pretty when it began, but were pretty ugly by the time it ended. They all had bloody mouths, swollen eyes and lumped foreheads. No telling how long the battle would have raged if Tito hadn't pulled up and caught the tail end of the fight.

"The fuck!" Tito fussed when he hopped out his car. Initially he came to watch the fight until he saw it was his family. He immediately sprang into action.

"Hey!" Unique fussed when he shoved her off his cousin. She tripped over the curb and landed on her back. She cocked her head curiously wondering how the same dude who laid her down and entered her could now push her down.

"Word?" Reign asked incredibly when he shoved her as well. They couldn't beat the woman alone so she wasn't going to fight a man, too. He balled both fist and stood next to his cousin in case they came for more.

"Chill, yo. That's some chick shit," Seven protested, but kept his distance. Tito was the man now and he needed to stay in his good graces. Plus, it was known that Tito was a killer and no one wants to get killed.

"Yo, y'all bitches ain't getting shit from me! Y'all better not even look at MY car again or I'm swinging on you!" Lisa promised. "If I even see y'all looking at it I'm swinging on you!"

"Swinging on who?" Simone wanted to know as she stormed out of her building, removing her own earrings. This wouldn't be the first time she and Unique fought a chick.

"Her, you, whoever!" she explained. Fake men giggled and

aimed their camera phones to record the action. Luckily, other men moved in and broke it up.

"Hold up. Y'all break this up!" Marcus said as he stepped in between them. He held Simone back from joining the fray.

"We good, ma. Come on," Unique called and came over to hold her mother back, too. She escorted her back upstairs with Reign right behind them.

"What was all that about? Girl, look at your face!" Simone fussed over her child.

"That bitch won't come off my brother's car!" Reign spoke up. "He put it in her name but she ain't pay for it."

"And legally it's hers. Nothing you can do," Bryan advised, coming from the bedroom. He too saw the fray pop off from the window but wasn't going out there.

"So, she just get to keep it? She probably got his money too!" Unique moaned.

"What money?" Simone wanted to know. The very mention of hidden treasure gave her vagina a throb. Reign gave Unique a frown that told her to shut her mouth.

"No money, ma. She just keeping what don't belong to her"

"Well let's get you girls cleaned up. I am a paramedic you know," Bryan suggested. Simone retrieved her first aid kit and ice packs.

Reign scrunched her face up as she watched him tend to her friend. Bryan looked at her chest as he cleaned her facial wounds. He was rock hard just from the proximity to the young girl.

"Come on, yo. Let's let my mom see. She's a nurse. A registered nurse," she said and pulled her friend away. Simone cocked her head curiously at the abrupt exit, but at least she and Bryan could pick up where they left off.

"Dang, you still hard?" she exclaimed when she reached down to his crotch.

"Cuz I been waiting to get back to this—" he said and

reached around to grab handfuls of ass. She went for it since she didn't know he was excited by her daughter.

"Well, here it is," she purred and turned around. He peeled her skin tight jeans down but not off and bent her over the sofa. Simone could only hope her daughter didn't come back while he wriggled his erection inside of her. "Ssss."

"I know right," he agreed and searched for his stroke. He knew he found it when she coated his dick in creamy white lotion. She was safe because Unique wouldn't be back for hours. He only needed fifteen minutes of back shots to send her over the edge. He was right behind her and erupted inside of her once more. He shook his head at his own foolishness that got him in the predicament he was in now.

"See, that's how you got us in this predicament now," she reminded and squeezed.

"Mmm, yeah," he said, taking a few last humps before pulling out. "Like I said. I'll take care of it. Just make the appointment and I got you."

"Got me what? What appointment?" she asked behind her then spun when she figured out where he was going. "I hope you don't think I'm having an abortion!"

"Well, yeah. I mean with your daughter pregnant and—" he said. Bryan was smart enough to keep being married to himself. He had a good woman at home with a good job who contributed to their good lifestyle. It should have been good enough for him to keep that good dick to himself but nope.

"And nothing! Man, you been busting in me raw and now you expect me to hop up on a damn table and have a baby sucked out of me! I wish I would go—"

"OK, OK. My bad," he surrendered with hands held high.

"Good. Now you can move in with us. We can be a family," she cheered and kissed his cheek.

"That wouldn't be such a bad idea," he said thinking of Unique. He enjoyed seeing her around the house in her little shorts and hope to see her in less.

"She wouldn't come off the keys ma," Reign whined when she came in. Her mother heard her baby and rushed over and tended to her wounds.

"That's OK. Let me see," Sharon said checking her lumps and bumps. She had just healed from the last beating but this one was far less severe.

"OK, your turn Unique. Let me see," she said and moved on to the next. "Ice pack and some cocoa butter and you'll be back. I gotta get ready for work."

"Like that?" Reign blurted out before she could catch herself. She popped her hand over her mouth but it was already out.

"I have mouthwash thank you very much," Sharon quipped and stepped down to her room.

"She been drinking again?" Unique stated the obvious.

"Yeah, I smell it," she said, twisting her lips. They weren't ones to talk since they planned to smoke as soon as she left for work.

"Ain't nothing changed. Stay in this house until I get home. You already got knocked up and beat up. No telling what else gonna happen next. I swear you kids—" Sharon fussed on her way out the door. "And you, if you going home, go home. If not, you keep your ass in this house, too!"

"Yes, ma'am," Unique said humbly. She couldn't help but smile and getting barked at. It was all love and she knew it.

"Talking all that shit, but you drunk," Reign mumbled once her mother walked out. For all her shit talking, she still hopped in the window to watch her to the bus. She was still grumbling until she saw the bus pull away. "Come on!"

"Why we going in here for?" Unique asked when Reign used a butter knife to unlock her mother's door.

"Cuz," she said, remembering Reef use to come in and out quite a bit. She assumed he stashed things under her nose and she was right. The first thing she spotted was a plastic bag from the coroner's office. They gave it to her when she claimed her son's body. It was still unopened so she opened it. "What the—"

"Nah?" Unique laughed when she came out with a key fob with a Mercedes emblem on it. Reign rushed to the window and pointed it up the block towards the car. She pressed the button and it hollered back with a quick honk of the horn and flash of the lights.

"Yeah bitch. If we can't get the whip you won't either!" she vowed.

"What we gonna do?" Unique laughed. She was down for whatever, whatever it was.

"I'on know but she not keeping the car. I'll burn it first," Reign said.

"But, we can't drive," Unique reminded.

"Yeah, I can! I seen my brother drive plenty of times. How hard can it be?" she said and went back into the bag. She came out with a couple hundred dollars covered in dried blood. Both girls began to tear up when they realized was it was. Neither wanted a dime of it, so it went right back into the bag.

———

Park on the next block, Lisa told JD so no one would see him pushing Reef's car. They still saw her when she walked with him into her building.

"Look-it" Jewel said, pointing at them.

"Where Reign?" Neta asked so she could file a foul report. She had a cell phone but still yelled her name. "Yo, Reign!"

"What now?" Reign asked when she heard her name. She stuck her head out the window to see what they wanted. "Sup, yo?"

"You know who just came home with some nigga," Neta told her.

"I'm on my way!" she said and rushed down stairs. It wasn't

the first time Reign broke her mother's rule about going outside, but she always felt a tinge of regret when she did. Neta filled her in over the next blunt.

"Yo, I was just around the corner with Seven and seen them pull up. Dude was whipping the whip!" Yvonne added.

Unique scrunched her face upon hearing Seven's name. She and Reign pretended not to care, but shot each other a glance that meant they were going to do something. After the blunt was done, they went back up and waited for the block to clear. They eased outside and over to the liquor store on Ogden Avenue. The clerk had no problem selling the underage girls 180 proof liquor. They came around the back way and found the car.

"If we can't have it," Reign began as they used the spare key to open the back door.

"She won't either," Unique finished as they poured the alcohol all over. They shared a quick snicker and lit their matches.

'WOOSH!' the fire grunted as it engulfed the interior. They would have loved to stay and watched it burn, but the orange glow lit up the night. They ran around the same corner and back into the building. Now Lisa could keep the car.

Chapter 16

"**G**et it, get it," Lisa called behind her as she gave it up. She dipped her back creating the perfect arch for back shots.

"I got it!" JD assured her as he dug her out doggy style. He was enjoying the sights, sounds and feel of the early morning back shots. He been wanted to get up in her guts, but he and Reef were friends and friends don't fuck their friend's girls. A real friend would rather let someone drink and drive than fuck their girl.

He ran out of condoms during one of their all night sexual sessions so he got one for the road raw. The baby cooing behind them in the crib was enough birth control for him to snatch out at the last second and bust on her back.

Shit, Lisa thought inwardly. Because of the warm globs of baby batter were landing on her back instead of in her womb. She needed to attach herself to the next baller and what better way to bag a baller than putting a baby on him. Next time, she decided. Since she knew there would be a next time after the way she put it on him last night.

"You want me to cook something for you? Since I kidnapped you and all," she offered with a giggle. She tricked him over to look at Reef's car and kept him all night. Once she got him she put that pussy on him to keep him.

"Nah, I gotta get home," he replied, sighing. He was hungry, but pretty sure his woman had cooked. She always did, even when he stayed out all night. His own car was parked on the next block too, but they took Reef's out for a drive to listen for the "problem" she reported.

"OK, papi. Let me walk you to your car," she offered since she decided to claim him as her own.

"Uh, sure," he agreed since he wasn't from around here. No one could report seeing him with a thot to his girl. She locked her arm in his to stunt for whoever was out. It was too early for many people to be out, but she still put on a public display of affection.

"Soooo, when I'ma see you again?" she asked when they rounded the corner. She saw the burned out shell of a car, but it didn't register as hers. The smell of fire and melted rubber still lingered in the air.

"Did you move the car?" JD asked, knowing he parked in that exact spot. It was directly across from his, so he was pretty sure. Especially when he saw the melted Benz emblem on the hood.

"No, I—Yo, my car! Them little bitches burned my car!" she shouted and spun on her heels. JD watched her ass as she stormed back around the corner. He shrugged his shoulders and got in his car to leave. He remembered hearing sirens when she rode him backwards and know he knew why.

"Uh oh!" Seven said when he saw Lisa stomping back up the block. She picked up and empty bottle and threw it at Reign's window. It shattered on the brick facade but still got the attention of the people inside.

"What the—!" Sharon fussed and came out of her room. Reign came out of hers as well to investigate.

"Reign! Get your ugly ass out here!" Lisa shouted when Reign came to the window.

"Bet," she replied and turned to get dressed to fight.

"Bet your ass!" Sharon cosigned and got dressed down, as well. She slipped on some jeans and pulled her Timberland boots tight. They met up at the door and rushed down the steps.

Lisa had put on so much, half the block was already out. Including Unique and Sharon, ready for battle. Tito jumped out some young pussy himself and rushed downstairs, too.

"Sup, cuz?" he asked coming to Lisa's side as the women converged.

"Yeah, what is up? Why you calling my daughter outside?" Sharon demanded.

"And threw a bottle at our window!" Reign added. Lisa may have gave her and Unique a run for the money, but now there was four of them when Unique and Simone joined them.

"Yo, I know you burned my car! I know you did that shit!" she shouted and tried to rush them.

"Chill, mami," Tito said restraining her. "Now, what happened?"

"I parked around the corner cuz—" she began then jumped completely over fucking one of her man's friends. "And they burned my car up!"

"My daughter didn't burn nothing!" Sharon said. She didn't know if she did or didn't and didn't care.

"Did you see her?" Tito asked.

"No, but I know they did it! They mad cuz they couldn't get it!" she snarled with fat angry tears running down her red face.

"Yo, I been down there all night and I ain't seen them," Seven said looking at Unique for points. He went in before the fire and wouldn't have seen them anyway.

"They wasn't even outside last night!" Neta piped up. When she stepped up the rest of the crew did, too. Lisa was a hot head, but realized a no win situation when she saw one.

"That's what's up. I got y'all. You think it's sweet? I got y'all," she threatened and stormed off. This would be a lesson to both girls to never let someone threaten you and walk off. "Hating asses!"

"Ain't no hating. We just don't like you," Reign laughed and the blocked laughed with her.

The sting of the laugher and loss of the car just made one dangerous enemy.

T he crowd broke up and went their separate ways. Reign and Unique stayed outside to kick it with their girls while Sharon went upstairs and started drinking. She was good and drunk by the time she went to work that evening.

———

"N urse Brown, make sure to give room 11 his meds, 13 needs his dressing changed, 21 gets insulin and 18—" the head nurse directed when Sharon reported for duty. She didn't smell like booze, but still had a boozy hue and sway about her. Her supervisor pursed her lips and asked, "Are you okay?"

"I'm great!" she cheered with a Tony the Tiger fist pump. She sure felt great since she was drunk. Her supervisor frowned as she wobbled away to do her job. It was only her excellent reputation that kept the supervisor from being concerned. She shrugged her shoulders and went to do her job and let Sharon do hers.

"Insulin," she sang as she breezed into the first room. The patient gave her a curious frown as she fixed a dose of insulin and injected him. She went to the next room and gave the woman her powerful pain pills. The elderly woman who suffered from dementia had fallen and broken her hip.

"OK, dressing change," she repeated when she got to room 18. She searched the patient, but didn't find any dressing to change. She shrugged it off as less work for her and went back on her rounds. She entered another room and announced, "Time for your insulin."

"Are you sure?" the patient asked as she injected him with a second dose of insulin.

"Well, I am a nurse," she giggled and gave him a shot. The man let it go since she was indeed a nurse.

"I didn't even know I was diabetic," he said and wondered aloud when she left the room. He assumed it must be pretty bad for him to get two shots within a few minutes. He wasn't and he just received a fatal dose of insulin. His blood sugar dropped until he dropped dead.

"Did I give you your meds already?" Sharon asked as she walked in on the elderly woman once more.

"No," she replied since it had been longer than her short-term memory could remember. She gladly popped another pill and laid back for a nap. This one would be a dirt nap because she wasn't waking up from this one. The overdose of the medication put her to sleep like a stray dog at the pound.

Sharon's work was done so she slipped into the nurses' lounge for a nap of her own. She stayed up drinking instead of sleeping and fell straight to sleep as soon as she stretched out on the sofa. A good sleep too, because the various alarms didn't even wake her up. People die all the time in a hospital but two at once who weren't terminal was strange.

"Where is Nurse Brown?" the head nurse called as she scrambled to save patients lives.

"I haven't seen her since she did rounds!" another nurse ratted. Two people who should have lived just died and wanted to make it known she had nothing to do with nothing. It took an hour to locate the sleeping woman since no one expected her to be sleep.

"I made rounds and they were fine!" Sharon exclaimed when she came on the scene. No one could challenge her excuses and explanations until the autopsies came back.

"Uh oh!" Reign said when she heard the keys enter the lock. The apartment was so full of smoke she didn't even bother trying to clear it. "My bad, ma. I—"

"Yo, if you not worried about smoking while pregnant why would I care about you smoking in my house?" Sharon said. "You gonna do whatever you want to do anyway. That's why you pregnant now."

"What you doing home so early? Thought you was doing a double," Reign replied to switch the subject away from herself.

"I had to come get some rest," she said, intentionally leaving out being sent home. A quick review of security cameras showed Sharon entered the lounge hours before she was found sleeping. It also showed her double back on her rounds, but lab results would have to tell the rest of that story.

"You do look tired." Reign said hoping her mother would go to bed. Instead, she plopped down next to her on the sofa. Reign popped up and headed for her room and dialed her best friend. Sharon reached for the half a blunt in the ashtray and lit it back up since her house was already smoked up.

"Sup, yo? What you doing?" Unique asked when she took her call. She assumed something was wrong since they just hung up from each other not long before. It was a school night so they both stayed in and stayed up.

"Nuffin, my moms just snuck up on me. Came home early and caught me smoking. Good thing I ain't had no nigga over here! I could have got caught getting my groove on!" Reign rambled.

"Girl, with who?" Unique laughed and cracked them both up. She perched up in the window to watch the block's night people do what they did. Reign did the same so they could share whatever they saw. "Uh oh, look-it."

"Girl, I see that ras clot, blood cot," she growled as Rankin's car eased down the block. It pulled in front of Tito's building and he rushed out and hopped in the passenger seat. She wasn't sure why she didn't say anything about him accosting her after the block party. She opened her mouth to say something now, but closed it. Meanwhile, Rankin had plenty to say down below.

"Whata gwan?" Rankin greeted and extended a rough calloused hand. "Every'ting irie?"

"Every'ting, I mean thing, good, yo," he replied, catching himself from mocking his accent since he got chewed out last time. Everything was good and he passed him a bag of cash to prove it.

"Yes, mon!" the dred laughed as he checked the weight of the money. It felt about right, so he tossed it in the back seat. He pulled the larger bag up front and handed it over. "Same ting."

"Bet," Tito said and prepared to get out.

"Wait mon. Where the gal dem? Reign she name?" he asked. It still wasn't adding up. The five hundred bucks was nothing, but his dignity was everything.

"Reign? You know she's Reef's little sister. She fine, but she ain't fucking," he said even though he still planned to fuck her.

"So why she tell me five hundred to go fuck? She took me up to the roof when I got jumped," Rankin said and heard how crazy it sounded. There was a brief silence as they both processed the obvious. Neither thought past it and the fallout that ensued.

"You see that? I wonder what's in that bag?" Unique said when Tito got out of the car and crossed the street to Lisa's building.

"Weed. He brought the money out in the smaller bag and got the weed in the bigger bag," she explained since she saw it done so many times by her brother. It could have been ten to twenty thousand dollars depending on much they sold.

"We need to get that bag, yo?" Unique said. She planned to get Tito back for pushing her down. She wasn't sure how but was sure he had it coming.

"We need to get both of them bags!" Reign added. Rankin

had it coming and she planned to get him, too. She pointed her finger like a gun and fired make believe shots at his car when he pulled away. Rankin getting his was a matter of when, not if.

————

"Yo, I'm giving you two pounds to bag up. I expect two pounds bagged up!" Tito warned sternly as he dug in the bag of weed.

"OK, yo. You don't gotta sweat me!" she fussed. She rolled her eyes and flipped her hair theatrically.

"Yeah, I do cuz last time it was a couple ounces short. And I'm paying you!" he reminded. Lisa had yet to bag a benefactor yet so he let her bag weed and cut crack for extra ends. That didn't stop her from pinching off the package for some personal.

"A'ight, yo. I got you, cuz. What ole Rankin talking 'bout?" she asked and grimaced at the thought of having sleep with him. He had plenty money but lots of ugly to go with it.

"Yooo, he think Reign set him up! She told him she would give him some pussy for five hundred, but the broad ain't fucking. As soon as they get to the roof, he get his head busted."

"By the little bald head one, I bet! They stay tryna jump somebody. Well, they better jump Rankin cuz he wanna do something to her. I caught him with her pinned up in her hallway after the block party. Reef was my man and all, but Rankin is the connect. We still gotta eat," he said. It was proof that loyalties don't last long.

"What was you doing in her building after the block party?" she dared and pursed her lips.

"Let me use your bathroom," he laughed and left.

"Let me use your phone," she snickered after he departed. She grabbed it from the table and quickly found Rankin's number. She sent the contact to her own phone and put it back.

"A'ight, yo. I'm out. Gotta spread this work out. I'll be back for that later and I'ma weigh it again," he reminded and set out to break the workers off. He still had to meet with Tariq and re-up with blow.

"Nigga, ain't nobody gonna take none of your weed!" she fussed. It sounded good but she was lying. Some chicks just can't be trusted and she was one of them. She already fucked several of Reef's friends and associates looking for her next meal ticket. She'd fuck Tito too if he hadn't been her family. She drew the line at fucking ugly Rankin but still gave him a call after Tito left.

"Here he come again," Unique said when she spotted Tito leaving his cousin's building.

"I see him," Reign said, locking in on the bag as he crossed back over to his own building. The line went silent as they both plotted on how to get that bag. Two salty chicks in search of a sweet lick.

Chapter 17

"Hello there, young man! Nice to see you awake," Sharon sang when she breezed into Kidd's room.

He still had tubes in his mouth so he blinked his reply. Sharon had been reduced to cleaning bedpans and taking rectal temps since the incidents. She was under an informal investigation until they got the autopsy and toxicology reports back. She could get a reprimand, lose her job or even go to jail. For now, she had to dump piss from pans.

"Uh oh!" she chuckled when she came across his early morning erection when she retrieved the bedpan.

"He's being released today," another nurse announced as she came in behind her.

"He is?" she questioned curiously. Kidd had improved dramatically and would recover, but he wasn't ready to go home.

"He's going to the jail hospital. The cop said he'll be our age when or if he gets out," she said as if he was still in coma and not listening.

Sharon could see the sorrow in his eyes, but there was nothing she could do to help him. She felt so bad that as soon as the other nurse left, she reached back under the sheets and found his erection. He blinked rapidly when she began to jack him off. It had been well over a decade since she last jacked her ex husband off in a prison visiting room. It was just like riding a bike and she quickly recalled how it was done. Kidd's eyes smiled when his legs began to kick. He busted a nut on her hands and she cleaned him up. That would be the last woman's touch he would have for years to come.

———

"I'm getting fine!" Unique proclaimed as she looked herself over in a full length mirror.

She wasn't showing yet, but her softball-sized breast were full and plump. Her hips began to spread as the girl transformed into a woman. She ran out of gel, but that was a good thing because she started wearing a short fro. Her hair could now grow since it was no longer glued down to her head. She stepped out of her room to find a shirtless Bryan in the kitchen. They both watched her eyes traced his chest, dropped to his crotch and then back up.

"My bad," he said, peering into her eyes and making her blush.

"Do you need school money?"

"Yes, I mean no," she answered truthfully then lied when she recalled her mother telling her she better not ask her man for money.

"Don't worry. I got you," he whispered and rushed off. He returned a moment later with a twenty. "Our secret?"

"Yes," she whispered back to match his whisper. He flashed his bright smile knowing if he could get her to keep one secret she would keep another. He watched her fat ass wiggle away and out the door. He realized he got hard and went to feed it to her mother.

"Look-it" Unique said and showed Reign the twenty. The both had less cash since Reef passed away.

"Where you get that from?" she asked hoping she could get one too.

"Um, Bryan," she admitted sheepishly like she knew it was wrong.

Reign raised her eyebrows but kept her mouth closed. They needed some money so she was in no position to complain.

———

"That's so sad. Poor baby," Sharon sang when Kidd was taken into police custody.

A detective walked along side his gurney as he was wheeled away. She wished she had time to jack him off once more before he left. Not just for him but because she enjoyed it, too. She found her sensible panties were soaked when she finished.

"The police said he killed somebody!" the other nurse revealed.

"That little boy? A killer? I don't believe it!" she said in his defense. The nurse badly wanted to let her know she was under investigation, but that would risk her own job. Sharon completed another day of limited duty then went home to drink. This was her new normal.

"Yo, I am soooo high!" Unique cheered into the phone. She and Simone just smoked a fat one and it was time for bed.

"Me too, yo," Reign replied, sitting alone in the smoke filled living room. Sharon was at work so she stretched out on the sofa and got blazed while watching some TV. "I'm 'bout to take my shower."

"Me, too. I'll see you in the AM, my bish," she said and clicked off. Reign rolled off the sofa and got up. She traded the TV for the radio and headed into the back. She stripped down to nothing and put her clothes in the hamper. Then spent a few minutes admiring herself in the mirror while the hot water built up enough to bathe.

"Mmm," Reign moaned from the satisfying combination of

the warm water and fragrant aroma of the body wash. She too started wearing her hair natural, so she washed it first. A glob of grease while wet would curl it up quite nicely. Once she finished bathing, she stepped out and dried off. She had just stepped into her room when she heard the front door open. She shook her head at getting caught, smoking inside once again.

"Shit!"

Reign shrugged since it was too late now and began to apply lotion to her skin. She heard footsteps coming down the hall and frowned. They sounded more like her brother than her mother, but that wasn't possible. She stood just as her bedroom door opened.

"Bumba clot! Lawda mercy!" Rankin said in a slow Jamaican drawl as he admired her fine brown body.

Reign was frozen in fear at the sight of the red-eyed dred in her bedroom. Her mind searched for the two guns she inherited from Reef. One was in her closet and the other under the mattress. Neither was any good to her right now.

"Fuck you doing in my house! Ma! Some man in the house!" Reign shouted in hopes of scaring him off. She was the only one scared and got even more when he began to laugh. A sinister laugh of someone who knew she was home alone and no one would be home for hours.

"No mon. Just mi and you mon," he said and parted his blackened lips into a smile. Reign was about to ask what he wanted but he answered by removing his shirt. His bird chest was covered in black curly naps that looked like taco meat.

"Fuck you doing, yo! Ain't nothing happening, my nigga!" she yelled as toughly as she could.

He just laughed once more and continued to undress. Things got urgent when he dropped his pants and revealed a massive erection. The big, ugly dick had a huge mushroom head and curved to the left. It looked about as thick as her forearm and she was determined to keep that thing out of her. It was fight or flight mode but he was blocking the door eliminating the flight option. She had no choice but to swing on him.

"Ya, that's what mi like!" Rankin cheered when she hit him with a two piece. He replied with an uppercut backhand that lifted her up and dropped her on her bed. She kicked at him with all she had, but it wasn't nearly enough. In fact, it actually worked against her. Rankin was able to grab each ankle and spread her legs wide.

"Blood clot!" he marveled once more as he looked between her legs. The practically new vagina seemed to beckon him, so he had to have a lick. He pulled her ass off the bed by her ankles and took a long lick on her labia.

"Chill, B!" Reign fussed as he began to eat her out. She fought against feeling good from his twirling and probing tongue. Luckily for her, he ate her so roughly only he got to enjoy it. He clamped his mouth over her lips and sucked her dry.

She realized she was powerless to stop him when he snatched her legs high and wide. He moved his massive meat between her saliva soaked lips and rubbed it. She remembered a victim once describing leaving her body when she was assaulted so she did the same. She mentally found a pleasant place and retreated to it. Only for a moment though because when he shoved himself inside, the searing pain snatched her back inside her own body.

Her only hope was that it would end quickly like sex with Kidd did. It was not to be though as the grown man pummeled the young vagina. Each stroke went deeper and deeper until he tapped on the bottom of her well. He was full of Red Stripe and spliffs and could go for hours.

"Sweet, young poom-poom," he moaned and stroked. Reign didn't suffer in silence. Instead she screamed bloody murder. Neighbors did hear her howls, but this was the Bronx AKA "mind your business".

Rankin began to growl and dig deeper inside Reign's insides.

Relief was strokes away as he neared the finish line. Now it was his turn to howl as he exploded on her cervix.

"Mmm. Sweet poom-poom," he moaned, dragging his dick around inside of her.

Reign huffed and puffed as if she completed a marathon. It was finally over, but he didn't get up. She could feel him throbbing inside of her as he came back to life and began to hump once more. "Mi a stay in this good poom-poom all night."

He didn't stay in it quite all night, but did literally beat it up for hours. Reign howled the whole way as she felt like she had a fire burning between her legs. Her only consolation of him repeatedly cumming in her was that she was already pregnant. Perhaps the only time in history a teenage pregnancy was a good thing.

"Grrrr, blood fire!" Rankin screamed and skeeted one last time. He grinded around in her like he did each of the other nuts he let loose in her young guts. This time he finally pulled his deflating dick out of her. He misunderstood the puddle of blood between her legs and under her. "You really was a virgin?"

Reign just snarled up at the man who just raped her. He smiled down at the damage done to her young poom-poom while she plotted on revenge.

"Time fa mi to leave, but I'll be back. Mi 'ave a key, ya know," he said, dangling her brother's spare key chain. She blinked her eyes trying to figure out how he had her brother's keys. It dawned on her that was the spare set he kept at Lisa's house. She did this. She set her up to be raped.

As an afterthought, Rankin dug in his pocket and dropped money on her dresser. Reign wanted to jump up and grab one, no both of the guns and let him have it as he walked out of her room. She wanted to, but couldn't move. She heard the door open and close behind him. He had the audacity to even lock it behind him when he left.

"I'm gone get you. Lisa, too. I'm gone get both of you," she vowed and sat up. She looked down between her legs to see if it really wasn't on fire. The blood tinged semen running out of her made her grimace in disgust.

She knew rape victims weren't supposed to shower so they wouldn't wash away evidence, but she had to get his seeds out and off of her. Besides, she vowed revenge and had no plans on making a report. Rankin didn't rape the cops. He raped her, so why would she call them.

"Oww!" she shrieked when she put a hot soapy washcloth on her battered pussy. She quickly realized cool water was the way to go. She only recently learned what the hot water bag hanging in the bathtub really was and filled it. She winced in pain as she used it to clean herself out. She would have to air dry when she stepped out so she didn't have to touch down there any more. Panties too were out of the question so she pulled one of her brothers T-shirt over head and got back in bed.

Reign spotted the wad of cash on her dresser and rolled back out of bed. It was over si x hundred dollars, but she still lifted her head in dignity and marched into the bathroom. She tossed the cash into the toilet and pulled the lever.

"The fuck!" she shouted and quickly dug it out before it swirled away. Rape or no rape, she needed that money.

———

"Mommy!" Reign shouted and rushed down the hall to greet her mother when she came in the next morning. She fully expected her mother but concealed a loaded gun under the sofa in case it was Rankin coming back for another helping.

"Why didn't you go to school?" Sharon asked as her daughter embraced her. She could tell from the hug it was more than just playing hooky. She felt guilty for hoping she miscarried, but it's how she felt. "The baby?"

"No, mommy. I just, I um, just missed you," she said. It was as close to disclosing what happened as she got. "We need to change the locks. I lost my keys!"

"Oh, man. We definitely have to change them with all these damn zombies roaming around now," she fussed. The recent addition of crack being sold padded pockets but some fuck shit always came with it. Just this morning she saw a crackhead jump out a car, spit a mouthful of cum on the concrete, and rushed down to one of the dope boys.

"We'll go when I get up. I—"

"No! Let's go now mommy!" Reign pleaded so desperately her mother squinted at her to see what she was missing.

"OK, baby. We'll do it now," she relented. She may have stayed up all night drinking but saw and heard her child's desperation.

Reign put her coat on and they headed up Ogden Avenue to the hardware store. Being a single woman Sharon could change locks and tires on her own just as quickly as she could make herself come on her own.

The locks were changed, but so was Reign. She didn't leave the house for days after the incident. Then it was only to school and back. She saw Rankin's car come and go as he did business, but he never came back.

"Sup with you, yo?" Unique asked when she finally came out her building for school. "Y'all go 'head so I can talk to my girl."

"Bet," Neta said as the two fell behind. They walked ahead and let the two catch up.

"Now, sup with you?" Unique repeated. "And don't tell me 'nothing' cuz I know it's something!"

"Yo, that nigga Rankin came to my crib the other night," she said and sighed.

"So, I know you ain't let him in?" Unique shot back.

"He had a key. My brother's key. He got it from Lisa," Reign said, trying not to cry. She failed but these were angry tears not sorrow.

"What he wanted?" she demanded hotly.

"He wanted to rape me. He did. It hurt so bad. That's why I ain't come to school. I could barely walk. I bled for days…" she relayed and drifted off. She snapped out of it when Unique spun on her heels and began to march back to the block.

"Where you going, yo?" Reign asked as she caught up with her.

"To go kill that ras clot, bumba clot dred!" she vowed.

"Chill, ma. We gone get him. And Lisa and Tito," she added.

"We gone get all they asses!" Unique cheered as Reign turned her around so they could go to school.

"We gone rock 'em to sleep, then rob them before we kill them. Yo, we gone kill them all!" Reign declared.

To Be Continued

www.ingramcontent.com/pod-product-compliance
Lightning Source LLC
Chambersburg PA
CBHW031129210626
46816CB00015B/1253